Profeta

by *Yuliya Dewolfe*

Illustrations by
Judith Mackay Stirt

FriesenPress

Suite 300 - 990 Fort St
Victoria, BC, V8V 3K2
Canada

www.friesenpress.com

Illustraions by Judith Mackay Stirt

ISBN
978-1-5255-4757-7 (Hardcover)
978-1-5255-4758-4 (Paperback)
978-1-5255-4759-1 (Ebook)

1. Fiction, Fairy Tales, Folk Tales, Legends & Mythology

Distributed to the trade by The Ingram Book Company

*This little book is dedicated
to my sensei Richard Kim,
who taught wisdom as well as knowledge.*

*Also to dear friends
Louisa and Abel Valério,
who showed me the beauty of the Azores.*

Fada

The stars, like unpiloted ships, moved slowly in their eternal patterns, floating deep in the uncharted silence of space. Their strange gravities pulled imperceptibly at the ocean's tides and at the destinies of mortal men. This veil of spangled movement paused for one infinite moment and formed an astrologer's Bowl pattern in our skies. Not a single star bore the symbol of earth in this formation, but only the symbols of air, fire and water.

Precisely at this juxtaposition of planets a female child was born. Her first lusty cry of life united her breath with the winds of the universe. Mother Moon, enchanted with the newly born promise of heart, threw of her mantle of clouds. She cast the naked splendor of her silver light straight into the babe's newly opened eyes.

Over the tiny pupils the moonlight washed, shimmering, searching out the entrance to the virgin mind. Penetrating inwards it ebbed and flowed. A sea of liquid lucidity, it sank still deeper, into the canals and recesses of the subconscious, finally finding its own silver reflected in the mirror of the child's soul. The soul drank in the moonlight as if it was spring water, changing forever the vision of the child. The cover of clouds then dimmed the luminous orb, but not before a silver brand had etched itself inside the psyche of the tiny infant. She gazed with unfocussed eyes at the strange play of light.

They named the child "Profeta".

She grew, experiencing the common magic of life that is the gift of childhood. Active, at times precocious, she showed no signs of being different. The adults thought of her as being perhaps a little more sensitive than other children. Some thought of her as having a rather poetic nature, for she seemed most content when she was exploring fields for buttercup chalices and blue forget-me-not star clusters. Thus she grew in the company of her family, close to the warm, brown and scented bosom of a gentle earth.

The growing years passed softly, floating away one by one like dandelion seeds.

The kaleidoscope of time turned and displayed a new design. Time also brought changes to Profeta. She had grown into a pretty young woman, adventurous, full of laughter, almost rebellious in her nature. She flaunted a bold and always curious spirit. A sense of loyalty and kindness lay in her heart, curled like a tender forest fern. This became apparent in her words and actions whenever any weak or beautiful thing lay open and vulnerable to the harsher elements of life.

Now it was, she started to experience subtle differences between herself and her companions. Unlike her friends, new knowledge and ideas were her fascination. Subtle stirrings moved their tendrils, misting vague memory like thoughts through her consciousness. Dreams came that changed the very basis of her reality.

Feelings akin to loneliness started to unfurl within her. The friends that surrounded her knew not the essence of her dreams, yet she could understand the essence of theirs. The plans and hopes of others were listened to with respect. When she spoke of her own visions, however, they would merely say, "Oh Profeta, these are but strange imaginings. They do not teach you the art of the kitchen, nor endear you to the safety and security of a young man's heart."

Her father, in turn, tried to dissuade her from speaking her thoughts.

Profeta

"Your images are an illusionary world, and if pursued they will lead to madness. You must not think of these strange silly things. Think of the earth only. That is where the essence of life is real."

Respecting his house, Profeta no longer shared with family and friends the questing in her soul. She did not mention the white angels in the sky. She now knew that others only saw white clouds. She did not sing the songs learned from the reeds, for she knew they heard only wind. She did not speak of her fascination with the moon but spoke of it only in terms of accepted astronomy.

Yet images continued to come to her with vividness and frequency. She tried in vain to thrust them away. They would not let her be. She began to spend more time alone, taking long walks. In this way she found some ease from the pretense that had been forced upon her, that her thoughts were the same as others.

At night she gazed at the stars, reading their maps. In the mornings she studied the rising of the sun. Her wanderings in the countryside began to unveil to her certain secrets which she found to be of great import.

The earth, she found, was not just there to place one's feet on. It had old knowledge of times gone by, and hints of times yet to be. A pebble, clutched in the hand, became the same as reading from a book on old civilizations. Everywhere the stone had been came to her mind with images as sharp as yesterday's events.

Listening to natures voice and studying the earth, she saw and sensed things that widened the rift of differences between herself and others. She learned to dance in the wind, and to cast spells using color and form learned from flowers and rainbows. Nature's constant and subtle symphony taught her the weaving of words into tapestries of comfort and hope that made her well loved by others, but still very much alone.

The canopy of night, sponged with so many stars, taught her the folly of vanity and the need to use all gifts lightheartedly and with good intent.

Thus her time was spent, fluttering its minutes in Profeta's mind like pale blue prayer flags in a bluer sky, unsettling her and filling her with unidentified yearnings. The odor of stagnation filled her senses, and she saw how all around her friends were settling in to the same moulds their parents had cast a generation before. She knew that contentment was not there for her. Instead a longing, as if for some long-forgotten land, gave her a restless heart known only to the souls of exiles.

And so it was that a late spring day, steeped in mauve perfume, lay its young hand inside Profeta's ribs. It cupped her beating heart and implanted its vernal energy. Drawn by an un-named call, Profeta's steps took her to the lilac dell, rich in the colors and scents of the season. All was quiet, drowsy, but pregnant with perfume. The air was sticky sweet, as though laden with honey. A bee droned lazily in the warm light, lulling her thoughts into silent empty spaces that only the blue of the lilacs filled. She lay on the grass, relaxed and peaceful. Her eyes were half closed, full of drowse.

A minute fluttering by her left shoulder gave her grounds to pause and examine a pale green butterfly that danced in the periphery of her vision. A tiny, curious ballerina, its zig zag flight explored her face and delighted her with its erratic dance. It came to rest on her right shoulder and spread its green wings to the light of the sun. Silver spangles wrought a strange metallic pattern in the fragile velvet. In an instant, light sparked off the silver, zinging into Profeta's unsuspecting sight. Sweetly it caught a silver sister-spark that lay hidden like a lost sequin deep within her being. The world grew silent. The butterfly let off a mist of diamond like dust, showering the air in reflected light. The light grew. It swelled, elongated, shaping itself into a long green and silver form. Gathering substance, it solidified into the physical form of a slender female.

This strange lady's graceful lines were clothed in green satin garb that draped in elegant folds down to satin slippered feet. A cloud of dark green hair the texture of seaweed fell to the curve of her hip. Translucent skin, like white-green grass that has been hidden from the sun, covered the sculpted bones. Lips and nailbeds showed the green of forest spruce.

The eyes. Oh but the eyes. They were strange indeed. They were slanted, heavy lidded, feline in appearance, and they had no discernible pupils. They appeared as multi-faceted spheres, and refracted emerald light like a well-cut gem.

Eternity let fly a single second as the apparition searched the open astonishment on Profeta's face. The green lady opened her lips in a smile, her breath scenting the air with emanations of new-mown hay and salt sea air.

"Don't be frightened, child. I am your green satin lady. I am known as Fada by some. I watched your birth, saw you grow, and now my darling one, I sense that it is time for you to travel. So go now, young woman. Say goodbye to your father's house and follow me on a journey."

These words were like a balm to Profeta's ears, as if somehow they had been long awaited. She took no pause to question their meaning. She only asked, "What shall I take for such a journey?"

The lady smiled so very gently before she answered. "You need bring only laughter, courage, yearning and a trust in me."

The words rang in Profeta's mind like wind chimes. Hearing their tinkling, she turned impulsively and ran back to her father's house. Flushed, excited and out of breath, she told her parents what she had seen and that the time had come for her to journey.

"Ungrateful child," Her father roared. "You will regret this foolish choice. When you do, do not think to re-enter this house, for I shall turn my back on you. You could marry well, find contentment. But no! You choose to pursue your strange ideas, fantasies, illusions. You will see! You will regret this! Then the time will toll too late for you!"

Hot and angry, his wrath tore at her.

Profeta's mother wept, and with frightened eyes she packed for her daughter a few things she might need. Silently, she gave her daughter a secret, hurried benediction.

Greatly saddened by her father's anger and her mother's pain, with moist eyes and determined feet, she turned back to the lilac dell. She knew she had to heed the urgent voice of Fada her green lady, that played so strongly in her ear.

When she arrived, Fada was there waiting. "Are you ready now?" she asked.

"Yes," came the simple reply.

"Then come, let us walk a while."

She took Profeta's hand. As she did, a movement filled the air. It seemed as though cellophane scarves were falling in the atmosphere. Together, one stride transported them through transparent and iridescent waves. They arrived into the yellow-green light of a forest that Profeta had not seen before.

The trees here were tall and still. Mystery hung from their branches, catching speckles of light. The softness of the moss that covered their path invited them to keep walking. They did so without speaking for a long time. All the while, the forest swayed around them as the wind blew. The patches of sky overhead, when visible through the trees, were cloudless and displayed a dazzling cobalt blue. The lady cast her gaze on Profeta's face and saw the shadow of melancholy there. She read Profeta's heart, then spoke. "Was it hard for you to leave your father's house?"

"Yes," was the quiet answer. I feel as though a small part of me was somehow lost. I wanted so much for my parents to bless me and be happy, but the shouting and tears have made me sad. I wish they could understand my reality, see with my eyes! Even if only for a moment.

Fada answered in a voice that was both soothing and patient. "That small piece you feel you have lost, Profeta, is the child within you. You worry that you have left that child behind, but you will carry her with you always. Without that child, our journey now would not be possible."

"As for the tears and the anger, they also are for the child within you, now lost to your parents. It is grief to them, and you must allow them their grief."

"As for your parents seeing your reality...I wonder dear Profeta, how many mirrors people gaze into before they find a true reflection of themselves and all there is around them. It is difficult to see how those images change from minute to minute, day to day, month to month, year to year, through all the cycles. It is hard enough for those like us, let alone for others to try and catch these swirling realities. If we put blame on them for this shortcoming, must we not also carry this burden?"

Once more they fell silent. They walked this way for several hours, Profeta wrestling all the while with the strange ideas of which Fada had spoken. Eventually, twilight caught them in its mauve fingers.

The lady stopped and turned to Profeta. She caught Profeta's hands in hers and searched her face. Fada smiled.

"It is time for you to travel on your own now."

"What are you saying?," cried Profeta. "I'm not ready to go on alone. Look, the night is falling. Where do I go, how do I get there?"

"Night, dear child, is only the same place without the day's light. You were ready to go alone when first you saw me and decided to follow. I may not walk with you, but where now is your trust in me? Remember to always make a friend of yourself. This will protect you from many dangers along the road, as well as give you good company. Take out the courage and laughter that you brought with you. Step surely, but with light feet."

She kissed Profeta on the cheek. Then, like a firefly, she enveloped herself in a greenish glowing light and disappeared. A slight wind blew through the tree tops, followed by silence.

Profeta stood alone and dismayed in the darkening twilight. A small silhouette, aching for the comforting lights of home.

She recalled her father's words and his anger then. This touched an anger in her own heart, but tempered by her mother's tears and benediction, the anger turned to courage. As the spark of courage grew and strengthened, it became a joyous excitement that filled her with optimism. She started to laugh, and somehow that laughter lightened her soul. She was sure now that Fada did indeed exist and could be trusted. She started down the path, alone now but stepping with light, confident feet.

A new moon, thin as a finger nail clipping, floated lazily into the night sky and dropped its velvet on the wandering girl. She found that she was getting tired and wondered where to spend the night. Darkness made her slow her pace and search carefully. She was seeking a sheltered spot. A slight bend in the little road presented itself. As she crested the curve, a small light seemed to make a flicker through the trees. Not daring to hope for some sign of life, Profeta searched for the glimmer between the dark trunks. It was indeed a light. The welcome possibility of a forest cottage gave so much comfort and courage that Profeta's steps willingly left the path and picked their way gingerly through the overgrowth to pursue the flickering promise.

After a quarter of a mile, through underbrush and trees, a sudden break in the wooden ranks thrust her unexpectantly into a grassy clearing. Here lay the answer to the mysterious little light. She was met by a scene that she was wonderfully and totally unprepared for. There, surrounding a warm fire, were a strangely garbed group of men and women. Eating and drinking seemed equally balanced with like amounts of laughter, talking, and voices breaking off into raucous songs.

The singing itself seemed to be led by a tall man, sturdily built, and bristling with energy. His hair was thick, long and flecked with silver. A speckled beard fiercely enveloped his chin in a hairy embrace. His blue eyes, shining with well-being, caught sight of the young woman standing with some uncertainty at the periphery of the fire's light.

"So, Madame has finally arrived," he bellowed out in a baritone voice. "Welcome to the warmth of our fire."

Not waiting for acknowledgement, he strode towards her, then proceeded to propel her by the elbow into the center of the circle of people. Bowing in exaggerated formality, he bade her sit on a tree stump.

"To hell with the formalities, park yourself on this and you shall meet the rest of the company. First, allow this one to introduce himself. Valerio, the adventurer, at your service."

He saluted and clicked his heels.

Profeta, too stunned to answer, sat on the tree stump and took the glass of wine he now thrust in her hand.

"Drink this," he ordered. "It will make you warm and lazy as a cat."

She did as he had suggested. Then, feeling rather more relaxed, she gave vent to her curiosity.

"How on earth did you know I was coming?"

"Madame, Valerio is no fool. He has friends in high places. My good friend Arruda here spoke to the pretty green one. She it was who brought us news of your arrival. So being the perfect gentlemen, which we no doubt are, we prepared a party in your honor."

He made a grandiose sweep of his hand, then turned away smiling. Leaving Profeta on her own, he started a rather flirtatious conversation with a pretty brunette who sat at his side.

A small man broke away from the group and offered Profeta a piece of meat from a roasting spit. She looked at him closely. He was a slight man, with dark, melancholy eyes and a face gentle and refined. The face was framed by dark hair, with a streak of silver at his right temple. Brown velvet garments seemed to hide rather than clothe his form. His words as he spoke were unrushed and well-modulated.

"I am Arruda, as you have already been told. I can see that you have travelled quite a distance already."

"How can you know this," she asked.

"I travel like the others here, and I study many things in many places. Tonight, I had the good fortune to speak with Fada. She told me that our paths would cross. She also asked me to advise you, if you had need of or asked for my advice. I am your good friend, in the truest sense of the word."

She glanced at him a little suspiciously.

"You will see, Profeta. Remember Arruda if you need a friend."

He then wandered off to join a quiet conversation with a group of the more serious people.

After that, many came to introduce themselves and made her feel welcome. Enjoyable hours passed, with many new faces who seemed to understand her without effort.

Later, Valerio turned his attention to her once more.

"Well Madame, in what way may Valerio be of service to you? Perhaps, oh droopy-lidded one, it would be best to discuss these practical matters in the morning, after some shut eye has taken away the effects of the wine."

He then dragged a quilt near the fire, rolled her up in it, then sang her a lullaby. He sang so loudly, and with such wild gestures, that she fell asleep in laughter.

The new moon waned in the sky. Night passed with its veils of wind. Gradually dawn on soundless feet crept so stealthily into the clearing that only the rising volume of the birds' orchestra finally broke into Profeta's dreamless sleep, asserting the new days arrival. She woke to find the clearing deserted, save for Arruda and Valerio.

"Where have the others gone?" she asked.

Arruda answered in his quiet voice. "They have gone to continue their own journeys."

Valerio presented her with a wooden bowl of strawberries and another with water. "For Madam's palate and toilette."

He waited for her to wash and break fast.

"Now for the matter which Madame must decide. Where would you like your journey to take you?"

"I hadn't given it much thought," she said. "I just knew that it was time to go. Is it so very important to know where you are going? Isn't it enough just to learn things and enjoy all that life has to offer. Surely that's enough."

"Whatever your journey may offer you," said Arruda, "know that there is always a price to pay. The more precious a joy, the more valuable a lesson, the greater the price. Are you willing to get what you pay for?"

"You are so cynical and morose Arruda," replied Profeta. Her voice held an edge of irritation.

"Not cynical my dear. I too love life, but have been journeying a little longer than you."

"Well, well," Valerio boomed out. "Sorry to interrupt such a pleasant chat, but I must be off for a short while. I shall be back presently. The lady, after all, needs to travel in style.

He crashed off into the woods and disappeared.

"Which direction do you plan to pursue," asked Arruda.

"Oh Arruda," answered Profeta with exasperation, "Whichever way my path should lead, I think I shall follow its natural course. Must I think out my journey so well?"

"Maybe not yet, for thought out journeys can often lead to frustration. However, the bearing is important for various spirits guard the four directions. One must always ensure that one is following an ascending spiral towards light. Many are the paths that twist and turn, only to bring us far from where we intended to travel. Hold true your course, Profeta. Then, no matter the byways, you will reach your desired destination."

"I don't yet know my destination," she answered, frustrated by his insistence in pursuing a conversation that was tiresome to her.

"That will reveal itself in good time, my dear, as long as you follow the proper direction."

"Oh Arruda," she laughed, breaking the seriousness of his tone. "Don't worry so about me. After all, I have seen Fada."

"True enough dear lady, true enough. It will be she who will guide your steps, not the heavy words of your friend."

So saying, he smiled, and they spoke of lighter subjects until they were interrupted by the shouts of Valerio. He then came crashing into the clearing, leading a beautiful grey stallion by a rope.

"A companion for Madam."

"Valerio, how did you manage this?"

"No problem, no problem, little one. You have to first be in need of a horse, then you simply find one. Either you find it, or it finds you. It matters not. Does he please you?"

Profeta's voice was full of delight. "Oh yes! But how shall I take care of him?"

"Silly girl, like you take care of any living thing. You tame him, feed him, pat his rump, blow up his nose, whisper in his ear and share portions of your life with him."

She gently ran her hand along the length of the animal's back, then laughed as he nuzzled her hair.

"See how easy it is," asked Valerio. "He will be loyal to you in your travels."

"As will your friends," added Arruda. "Remember, you have friends if there is need of them."

"But can you two not join me," she cried. "You two have been so good to me. It would be such great fun to travel with friends."

"Madam, Valerio is sorry. He must be off on his own adventures, and to do so he must travel alone. It feels better on his skin that way."

"As for me," spoke Arruda, "I have much work to do. Many things have not yet been recorded."

"But why cannot friends travel together?"

"Oh, but they do," said Arruda. "They travel in parallel lines. They are close by to help you if you require it; or to share a joy with if that is your wish. It is enough to know that somewhere they exist, and our paths may unexpectantly intertwine with theirs at times. However, the important journeys are for one alone. Only then do they truly become our own journeys. Friends provide a precious rest when we get travel worn, or when there are stories to compare. They give us the gift of gracious healing if some mishap has left us with grievous wounds. They come flying in on the wings of love, if we are open to giving. Therefore, do not be afraid to go on alone Profeta. Remember to make a good friend of yourself also."

Profeta picked up the last sentence and lay it to the side of Fada's words. They sounded in harmony.

"Very well, my friends," she smiled. "I shall be off."

The three of them set to gathering a few essentials together. Valerio then helped her onto the horse. She leaned down, kissing each on the forehead.

Then, digging her heels into the horse's sides, she galloped gayly out of the clearing. She followed a path turning East through the woods, turning back but once to call out, "Thank you. I do so love you two."

The men glanced at each other, smiled, and then made preparations for their own imminent departures.

Profeta followed the forest path, with its intertwining byways, for many years. During this time, she met with many like herself. From time spent with them in conversation, she learned that some journeymen and women were strong and individualistic, others simply rebellious.

Still others seemed tired or weakening from years spent on the road. These were the ones who had lost their direction.

She came to know the main shelters, the most hospitable dwellings.

She also came to know her horse, Slate, as she had named him. With him she exchanged loyalty and respect, forming a strong bond with this animal.

She also grew to feel at home in the forest. It held for her her own reality. Here, people understood the things she spoke of. She no longer had to hide her own feelings and thoughts. Any need for pretense was gone.

There were times also spent in the company of her friends, Valerio and Arruda. Between travels and business, all three took time to develop a strong friendship, unhampered by time spent away. The three were always grateful when paths crossed, relaxing and laughing in each other's company.

Thus, the roads molded her. She learned the art of extricating herself from unpleasant situations, and to listen to the sound of her own heartbeat. She found the friend within herself. By protecting this friend, she came to know her own self-worth.

The seasons revolved, turning time on their mill wheels, flooding the land with another late spring. Once more, a new moon greeted Profeta. She found herself in a part of the great forest that was not very familiar to her. Leading Slate through the trees, she was seeking a shelter in which to spend the night. Low hanging branches caught at her hair.

She found herself unexpectedly walking into a quiet, abandoned orchard. Barren trees, like dark skeletons, loomed up out of the darkness. They were decorated sporadically with tiny white blossoms that shone under the little moon.

Shaking off a slight feeling of apprehension, she untethered her horse and allowed him free grazing. He never wandered far from her.

She wrapped herself snuggly in her cotton sleeping quilt, the new moon reflecting in her eyes, and waited for the thin light to bring her dreams.

Her eyes were filling with drowse when a small rustling sound, like a dry leaf scraping along on an unpredictable wind, scratched at her consciousness. Slightly startled, she sat up and listened intently for sounds reminiscent of night animals. This uncanny rustling had about it a very different quality.

She looked to her horse for clues. He stood rigidly, nostrils flared, smelling the night. Profeta stood up stealthily next to Slate's head. She strained in the direction of the unfamiliar sound. It seemed to come from a very tall clump of grass that appeared to move and swell darkly.

She stifled a gasp of horror as her eyes found the source of the rustling. Small, ugly creatures, bony and naked, were scuttering about in the grass. The new moon's light reflected their fish-belly white flesh. They had spiny ribs and pendulous breasts. It was with shock that Profeta realized they were all of the female gender. Their feet and hands were gnarled and calloused. Skull like faces, with bulging eyes full of mockery and evil, sneered greedily as they ran back and forth through the shadows.

Slate reared and snorted, and Profeta tried to calm him. She jumped at the sudden sound of a silken voice behind her.

Profeta turned. "Who are you," she burst out angrily, a slight edge of fear pulling at her throat.

"My name," said the man, "is Silvamalo. I have heard of the beautiful way that you dance, and of your friendship with Arruda and Valerio. Do not be afraid, for I am your friend also."

"What from hell are they," she asked, pointing a trembling finger at the miniature horrors.

"They are Liliths, and they will not harm you. If they displease you, I shall send them away."

Silvamalo's tall, lanky frame moved toward the grass, whispering words she could not decipher. The Liliths stared at her malevolently then sulked away, scurrying like malformed centipedes.

"They live here," said Silvamalo matter-of-factly. "Come, come. If you don't like them, you needn't sleep here. I have a dwelling not a moment's distance away."

Noticing her hesitation, he added, "Arruda and Valerio are also my friends. Is this the horse they gave you?"

He put a slender-fingered hand on the horse's neck. Slate pulled away but became still as Profeta spoke soothingly to him.

"Why have I not heard of you before?"

"I am a loner," he answered. "Many people do not know of my existence, and I prefer it that way. Don't be so very suspicious, Profeta. I offer you a night's shelter, that is all."

Not relishing a night spent in the orchard, and feeling somewhat tired, she made up her mind after a moment's indecision.

"Very well," she conceded. "Lead the way."

She thought for a moment that she had seen a flash of green at her shoulder, but her turning eyes caught only a tree bough. Thinking that she was acting silly, and a little ungrateful for the kind offer, she set of to follow Silvamalo.

An easy grace to his movements complimented the curl of his hair, which fell to the collar of his dark green cape. His face seemed sensual, almost boyish at times, as he turned to smile reassuringly at her now and again. She followed his sure-footed steps, admiring the soft, black leather boots that he wore.

They walked down a path she had not known existed before. Presently, they came to the mouth of a yawning cavern that was carved into a dark hillside. He noted her faltering and turned to her, smiling.

"It is perhaps a little humble in its appearance on the exterior, but I think you will approve of it when you see the décor inside. Don't worry. You can sleep on my bed, alone. I will be quite comfortable on the floor."

Again, she thought herself foolish for mistrusting him. She tied Slate to a nearby tree and entered the cave. Inside it was of large proportions. Strange, gilded, thorny roses climbed up the rock walls. Petrified trees decorated the ceiling. Silk covered cushions and low carved wooden tables were scattered throughout. On one side was a huge bed, piled high with furs. All was bathed in a bluish light.

"It is beautiful," said Profeta. "How long have you lived here?"

"For a while now, but you look tired. Sleep now, and we shall talk of this in the morning."

He looked at her intently, silently, then walked to the bed and drew back the top furs.

"I hope you will be comfortable on the pillows," she said.

He caught her pointed remark. With a wry smile, he said, "I shall be indeed."

She walked to the bed and climbed in under the softness of the furs. "Thank you for your kindness, Silvamalo."

"Go to sleep," was all he answered.

Indeed, she soon fell into slumber, though her sleep was not a peaceful one. Bizarre dreams came to her. She seemed to hear far off rustling and quiet weeping, as if coming through a fog. Was it her own voice she heard? Then, Silvamalo's voice seemed to float in, soothing her. Finally came a blackness with no dreams. Thus, she spent a fitful night.

When morning came, she woke to find Silvamalo looking at her from across the room. "I think you had nightmares, so I watched over your sleep."

She felt slightly disconcerted by the intensity of his gaze. Sensing this, he pulled his eyes away from hers.

He prepared for her a marvelous breakfast, showing thoughtful touches in the laying of the table and he ministered graciously to her needs. He talked to her all the while in his liquid tones, and told her tales that pleased and amused her. Profeta found herself strangely intrigued and drawn to him.

After spending the entire day talking and laughing with him, her compulsion to get back on the road had faded somewhat. She danced for him in the evening, warming to the delight she saw in his face as he watched her. That night, she agreed to stay and visit with him a while longer.

The days began to pass, uncounted. She started to trust him, and told him of her travels. His personality fascinated her. He was like a mirror of water, understanding all that she told him. He seemed to have shared similar thoughts, experiences, and emotions. When they talked, his eyes would never leave her face, drinking her in. His deep gaze kept drawing her out towards him.

As Profeta stayed longer and longer, she began to be unaware of time and space. Her entire being seemed caught up in the web of his eyes. Days and nights became indistinct. Her life began to revolve around those eyes, dilating and expanding. They encompassed her, and made her feel beautiful, sensual, precious.

She did not recognize precisely when friendship and laughter turned to a different feeling. When small touches became intimate caresses. When the blackness of his eyes entwined with the silver fibers of her mind, inking out her own light.

Eventually they became lovers, and she realized how lonely she had been before him. All of her thoughts now became centered on him. Happiness and peace was found only in his company. She forsook the images of herself, and saw as real the reflections of herself as mirrored in his eyes. She gave him all her gifts of loyalty and warmth. She opened herself completely, entrusting him with all of her happiness. So Silvamalo trapped her spirit with shows of gentleness and love.

Secure now in the knowledge that she could no longer see anything but what he wanted her to see, he started to slowly drop his disguises. The changes were so small at first that they were barely perceptible to Profeta. He began to treat her with less consideration, while asking far more from her in return, until it was she that felt inconsiderate. He no longer complimented her, even when she danced for him. Soon, she lost confidence in her own beauty and lost her joy in dancing. He feigned hurt and pain when she would go out riding her neglected horse, saying that he felt a panic when she left him. Feeling guilty for causing him such pain, she stayed longer and longer in the cavern, trying to amuse herself for his sake. She gradually became a prisoner there, shackled by her own blind feelings and emotions.

Silvamalo, meanwhile, began to spend more and more time in the woods away from her. If asked for an explanation, he would only stroke her face lovingly and answer that he was working on a gift for her.

His explanations turned to accusations of her short comings.

"I work hard because I love you," he would tell her, "but you are not loyal or trusting. Otherwise you would not question me!"

Open and vulnerable to his words, Profeta searched deep in her heart. Being loyal and trusting, she saw there the imagined short-comings. After this, she never questioned his absences. She blamed herself, and shriveled more and more inside, changing from a happy person who loved to laugh into a gaunt woman with sad eyes.

He came back one evening in the company of the Liliths. They pranced around the cavern and snickered darkly at Profeta's pain. They fawned openly on Silvamalo. Profeta withdrew to a corner in silence and waited for them to leave.

I despise them, Silvamalo. They disgust me. They are the antithesis of all that is light in life and being. They grovel in front of you and you allow them to paw at you. You give them the power to laugh at me, and all we hold sacred between us." Her eyes were wet with tears.

"Profeta, it is not their fault that they are unlovely to look at. I am the only person that they can communicate with, for I do not look at them with revulsion. Surely, my sweet, you are not jealous of them. Come, come, my love. Try to be a little kinder.

So the matter was closed. This left her feeling that she was not as compassionate as he. Thus, the light of self-knowledge was once more dimmed by his manipulative words of illusion. The friend she had found within herself faded still more, and she began to show spiney ribs and a faint bluish hue. Not enough yet to be perceptible to the human eye, but there to be seen by those who could read the human soul. Silvamalo had this gift. The start of this transformation made him smile; a knowing, power-lusting smile.

As for Profeta, long hours were spent in sleep. Tiredness robbed her of the strength to see the center which was fast becoming a hollow cave in her spirit. Afraid she was to see the harshness of reality that the light of truth would bring. Fatigue drained away any prospect of climbing out of the deep melancholy that had overtaken her.

One cool autumn morning, waiting alone once more for her dark-eyed lover to return, she heard a knock on the door of her wistful reverie.

"Who's there," she called out. No one had ever come to visit before. Valerio's voice came echoing into the cavern, singing a loud serenade.

Profeta flung the door open in happy amazement and was greeted by the site of Valerio and Arruda.

"My friends, my own dear friends, I have not seen you for so long." She laughed and hugged them closely to her.

Valerio held her off at arm's length.

"We came to see how Madame has been keeping. We too have missed your company. It seems that Madame has become a skinny wench. Where have your curves gone to hide? Have they run in fright from Valerio, the great admirer of the female form?"

"Oh Valerio, I have only lost a little of my fat." She tugged self-consciously at her dress.

"You two must stay until Silvamalo returns. Since he is a friend of yours, I am sure that he will be glad to see you."

"We are indeed acquainted with him," Arruda said quietly. Noting the shadows in her face, the change in her heart's light, he did not smile.

They sat and talked a while. Profeta extolled the virtues of her lover, too proud to tell of her confusion. She was unable to hear the twisted messages of sorrow her own mouth was uttering in the false air of gaiety she tried to portray.

A long time passed and Silvamalo had still not returned. Valerio got up to leave.

"Well Profeta, where is this illustrious man of yours? Is it his habit to leave you alone until night fall?"

This was more a statement than a question.

"Well, you know, he has business in the forest," she said defensively.

Arruda searched her reaction briefly before replying. "Profeta, my friend. I shall give to you the advice that the Green Lady once gave to me, when I was younger. Remember the price that one must pay for lessons learned. Remember, lessons that reveal the truth of reality are worth any price, for they bring freedom for the friend inside yourself. Never be unkind to that friend, for if you are, you shall lose self-worth. You will become one of the Liliths, rustling in the night. They were no different than you at one time. You must trust yourself, not the reflections that you see in another's eyes. Don't just hear words that please you, but observe the actions of the body itself."

"What exactly are you trying to say Arruda? Are you comparing me to those horrible creatures?"

"They were once beautiful as well, but they sold out their spirits because they grew tired, or fearful or greedy. All that remains is what you see now. There is within each of us many a fantastic creature, or a monstrosity, waiting to hatch if the right soil is found to seed itself," he replied sternly.

"Arruda, I don't understand. What have the Liliths to do with me? Why are you being so unkind?"

Valerio quickly interjected, trying to dispel the tension in the room.

"Valerio and Arruda must be off to visit the roses, with their pretty little faces that cup the sun. They are like budding virgins, and remind Valerio of times gone by."

Saying this, he let go a tremendous sigh.

Profeta, feeling angry and disturbed, was grateful for an end to this conversation. She rose to see her guests off.

They embraced her at the door, mounted their horses, and began to gallop off. Just before the bend in the road hid them from view, Arruda turned in his saddle and shouted out into the crisp air, "Don't be fooled, Profeta. Investigate his nightly business, before it becomes to late for you. Be strong for the sake of your soul."

The sound of the receding hoofbeats sounded a sudden drum of fear in Profeta's mind as she turned back to the cavern.

Automatically she started to tidy the room, hoping to thrust away the worms of doubt that niggled at her mind. Arruda's words, however, welled up in an awful wave of anxiety. She lay down on the fur piled bed and allowed the wave to crash over her. The fear took her into twisted inner paths that were uncomfortable to walk in. She reviewed the months of happiness that she had found with Silvamalo, but her heart constricted when she saw that the joy of the past had become but an illusion. She saw then how her strength had ebbed, and how she had become too tired to see anything but his mirror eyes. Those eyes made her see only reflections of what she had desired.

Silvamalo had used his power over her heart to make her believe that she was unkind, jealous and disloyal. All qualities that she had always found repulsive.

Panic set its cold hand inside her ribs, and she saw that the little friend within her had become a far sadder creature than the one she had taken with her on the beginning of her journey into the forest.

She now bore a faint but undeniable resemblance to the gaunt, shriveled structure of a Lilith.

The pain to be paid for learning the truth made her want to deny it. The pain of seeing that precious gift of self, given so willingly and with such trust, only to be treated so poorly. It was as if it had been worth nothing, and brought such a hurt to her. Silvamalo's illusions were far more comfortable than the bright light of reason and reality? Maybe, just maybe, oh please let it be, Arruda could be wrong.

"Why did my friends leave me to face this test alone. I am no longer strong enough to see beyond the words. I only feel loneliness seeping into my bones."

The strange, gilded roses on the walls bore silent witness to her anguish. Her frightened words hung darkly in the dank atmosphere, their syllables muffled by the face of the patient rock wall. Her eyes finally closed in a troubled sleep.

Ah, but time had some kindness for Profeta. Fada came gently into her dreams, bringing with her the cool comfort of forest shade. She visited the scorched mind and touched a silver strand that lay forgotten in a corner, dark with sorrow. A long-lost trust in the Green Lady remained hidden away in that same corner.

Silvamalo, the Lilith maker, returned to his domain as twilight danced in maroon shadows. He looked approvingly at Profeta's strained face. Soon now, he would finish what he had begun, capturing another female with his words. He would rob her of her strength, transferring her will to his with false love and pretty illusions.

"Wake up little one," he whispered. I have only an hour to hold you, for I must be off again. But oh, how I have missed you."

"I have been thinking wrongly," she told herself. He is good and caring.

"Silvamalo, please don't go. Stay with me tonight. I need you. Can we not sit and talk of times gone by?"

His answer was to push her hand away.

"Don't be silly, Profeta. You know I must be off. Remember, my business is for the both of us. Soon you will see my fine surprise and will be happy. Then we shall have all the time we want to enjoy ourselves, as lovers should."

Profeta fell silent. A tightness fixed itself in a band around her chest. Sad and empty, she watched as he prepared for another departure. She kissed him with cold lips and walked him to the door, taking note of his disguised impatience to leave and the direction in which he had set off.

Profeta dressed quickly. Her shaking hands saddled Slate.

Quietly, she set off in Silvamalo's wake. His imprints had been left on the dewy grass, making his tracks easy to read. She rode silently, slowly, following the signs. Her mind was full of foreboding, but within was lodged a thin quill of hope. Her opposing emotions made her tremble, letting in the chill night breezes. She drew her cape tightly around herself.

The tracks led her on a twisted course through the trees, back to the abandoned orchard where their first meeting had taken place. It seemed to her so long ago.

Profeta's concentration was pulled from introspection, into the reality of her immediate surroundings. Hidden in the shadows of a clump of barren trees, horse and rider sifted forward through the darkness that lay like a thick blanket on the orchard air. Quiet, all was quiet. A scuttling sounded once, then silence again. Only the wind wept in the empty branches. Moments passed.

A sound caught her ear then, an unmistakable rustling from the opposite side of the field. Pale as marble, she looked for the source of the now familiar sound. Dim shadows writhed like snakes in the grass, hidden by darkness and distance.

With no forewarning, a full moon slid noiselessly from behind a cluster of clouds. All that had been hidden by darkness was now etched in silver.

In stark outline, there was Silvamalo. He lewdly caressed a breast that drooped pathetically from one of the Liliths, while the rest of the cadaverous creatures snuffled and nuzzled their master's thighs with obscene intent. Silvamalo's features, sharpened by moonlight, glowed with lust and a fanatical love of power. His greedy heart was reveling in it. He suckled like a leech on the writhing bodies around him, drawing strength from manipulating any bit of gentleness or passion they showed towards him in his frenzy.

She felt a sudden pity for the Liliths then, but it was drowned out. The falsehood of the loving intimacy that he had pretended to share with her ripped into her heart, leaving a clot of rage that flashed through her. Illusion was broken by the iron fist of truth. Unrelenting fury spilled into her hollow core, reckless and vengeful.

Digging her heels into Slate's sides, she broke into full gallop across the orchard, intending to trample her unmasked lover.

Silvamalo's ear caught the thunder of the hoofbeats. Startled, he saw his victim streaking towards him, danger riding on the horse's hooves. He realized then that she was no longer in his power.

He sought out Slate's eyes. Fixing on them, he threw off a dark energy at the horse that caused him to rear up in a dead stop.

In vain, Slate tried to push past the shield that Silvamalo's evil had created. He pawed at the air with no effect.

Enraged, Profeta shrieked into the gathering wind, "Silvamalo, you spawn of Medusa. I see past your eyes and your words. I curse you, parasite, you vampire of women."

He laughed, unctuously, drawing his cloak around him.

"My dear Profeta, it was you who tricked yourself. You wanted to see your little soul reflected in my eyes, and also it was you who wanted to believe in your silly romantic illusions."

The scorn in his tone vaulted her into hatred, and at last exposed the strength of her will. Screaming an animal sound, she burst through the force that his black energy had created, for righteous anger had power over this shield. Coldly and methodically she veered Slate's strong frame towards him.

Sensing a new danger, he raised his hand again and threw a flashing pain across the air, forcing Profeta to slump over, breathless.

She glared at him through slitted eyes. Again, she urged her horse forward.

He let fly a cold pain that split in jagged lightning flashes across the air. It snaked into her temples, bursting a star of agony inside her head and convulsed her into blackness.

Slate, panicked by the limpness of his rider, bore down on Silvamalo with increased speed.

The Magician again hurtled hatred across the air, aimed straight at the animal's loyal heart. It exploded instantly. Blood spewed from Slate's mouth. He hit the ground, throwing Profeta clear of his thrashing, then mercifully lay still.

The destruction that their master had caused sent the Liliths into squeals of glee. They swarmed over Profeta's still form, as well as the dead horse, chortling in victory.

Silvamalo sauntered over to where Profeta lay. He looked at her with cold, sardonic eyes.

"Well you are, after all, a weakling. Not enough of a challenge for me."

Profeta lay unconscious, not hearing his words.

Calling his horde to his side, Silvamalo swaggered back to his cavern followed by his unlovely troop.

Profeta lay quiet, floating in a void of blackness. A land of no memory, no pain. A velvet sea of deep forgetfulness. The faintest vapor escaped her lips and hung in the morning mist, then mingled with the saltless tears of dew. It was the morning's weeping that revived her. It beckoned her to an unwelcome feeling of emptiness. Unable to move, she turned her head and tried to focus on a shadowy figure that stood over her.

Arruda's concerned voice edged towards her consciousness.

"I was afraid that the unrest the night wind spoke of was this damage. Luckily, I was not far gone yet. Hush now. Don't try to speak. Thank Fada for sending me back just in time."

He gathered her up and gently lay her in front of his saddle. Then they left the fateful orchard and galloped to a place Arruda knew for healing. As the light of the morning danced around them, a streak of silver glistened softly as a spider's web in Profeta's long, damp hair.

The Warrior

The sea, with its green message of new beginnings, danced in ebb tides on the shore. The rhythm of the waves had sculpted the sand into gentle forms, echoing the harmony of its music. Patience and persistence used liquid hands to shape the immovable as sharp edges became softly rounded. Bygone disruptions, traces of the Earth's disharmony, all washed into oblivion by the gentle erosion of sea foam.

It was here by the water's side that Arruda lay Profeta down on a thick bed of dry seaweed to begin her healing. She lay as if sleeping for several days, falling in and out of waves of darkness.

Slowly, the hum of the ocean's swells engendered an echo inside her breast. The monotony of the sound enticed her heartbeat to find its regular rhythm once again. Salt spray, drying in minute crystals on her forehead, started to numb the grief in her mind. Billowing breezes, , subtly scented with life, brought to her gusts of strength.

Arruda was soon joined by Valerio. Together they sat a silent watch like sentinels, protecting her and bearing witness to her mourning.

Eventually, she roused. In a flat voice she asked, "why, oh why did you not come to tell me the truth in the very beginning?"

Arruda placed a gentle hand on her shoulder.

"Had we come earlier it would have been too soon for you to listen. You would have thought our interference to be the cause of your pain, and would have then turned still further from the truth.

Timing is important for all warnings. It is only through your own eyes that you can see the shine of reality. You cannot borrow someone else's eyes. In the end, you were strong enough to seek it yourself, and to pay the price."

"What have I bought at such a cost," she cried. "Only pain, shattered dreams, and the death of my beautiful Slate."

"Dreams don't shatter so easily," said Arruda. "They only change form and become the makings of a future reality."

He took her hand.

"A comfortable illusion grows and solidifies on us like a second skin. If it gets peeled away, there is great discomfort in the peeling. However, if we are allowed to heal properly, we may find that the skin we have lost was like a prison. It is reality that gives us true freedom."

"A little snake may feel displeasure shedding the old patterns of its skin, but the truth is that the old one was too dull and tight."

"Is not the whole process a signal of growth, fresh color in old designs? Is it not a joyful event?"

Profeta fell silent for a time, seeking out the thin line where the sea met the horizon. Eventually, she turned once again to Arruda.

"So now, my friend, advise me. What must I do with all my sorrow."

It was Valerio who answered her this time in a surprisingly quiet voice.

"Madame, first I must teach you to fight. Then you will better understand wherein your true enemy lies. After, Valerio must take you to meet an old acquaintance of his. We shall start all this in a week's time, when hopefully your returning health has put a tinge of color in your cheeks."

As he had predicted, the time came when Profeta became stronger. Valerio started her on a disciplined course of physical activity. Each week, he stepped up the demands on her body, making her gain in strength and stamina as she worked hard to meet the challenge.

She became more flexible, and her lines became better defined. Her strength pleased her.

Her grace and confidence in movement was enhanced as well. She began to dance once more at night, much to the pleasure of her friends.

Valerio soon introduced her to the art of fighting with a wooden staff. In mock battles with him she polished her skills and developed new techniques, exhilarating in the clash of wood on wood. All of her anger and bitterness was given full vent in this manner.

Always, Silvamalo and his lies were the enemy she sought to destroy. The image of the dark magician floated, always superimposed over Valerio's form.

Valerio never let her win. The frustration of always being defeated was the whetstone for honing her skills.

One morning, Arruda left his scrolls to sit and watch them duel a short distance away. With speed and control, Valerio opened his attack strongly and in full earnest.

Profeta once more saw the face of Silvamalo before her. With anger and a snarl, she defended herself strongly, but Valerio now started to hit out at any opening with greater force than he had used previously. All of her concentration and strength had to be pinpointed in each block. Silvamalo's face faded, and all that was left was the reality of blows that came at her and the sharp focus of her targets. She began to fight with relaxed coldness and steely intent. Only body, mind and eyes. No anger now, just points of focus. No fear of being hit, just intention of targeting. Blocking, blocking, thrusting, being blocked.

Suddenly, an opening. A deep thrust strait to the target. With sharp awareness, she struck a blow straight at Valerio's heart, minus one inch.

They stood frozen in place, the point of her staff poised accurately one inch from his warm flesh.

Profeta let out a strong cry of triumph and threw her staff in a spiraling arc against the smiling sky.

"Valerio, Valerio, the enemy, the enemy," she exclaimed. "The opponent is none other than oneself. It's our own devils that we must overcome, our own devils that are the hold the magicians have over us. It is all in our own minds. Leave behind our own stories, focus, and they are gone."

She let out another whoop of triumph.

Valerio, flushed and dripping with sweat, made his staff twirl like a windmill.

"By God Arruda, crack open a jar of wine. This Madame has now become a formidable warrior!"

"A warrior newly found indeed," mused Arruda, "but still untried in true battle. However, a warrior just the same."

Profeta laughed. "Arruda who sent you as a plague to me, to never let me revel or rest in my small triumphs without words of caution? Bring out that golden pear liqueur that you have been so protective of and let us celebrate."

Arruda walked smiling to his pack and withdrew a clay crock.

"So, Profeta, your anger has at last turned to triumph. Tell me, how does it feel inside your ribs now."

She replied, "I must confess, my friend, that there is no more pain. Now there is just a small nut of bitterness."

"Bitterness, bitterness, you say," boomed out Valerio. "Doesn't Madame know that even a little of such poison will ruin the lines of Madame's face. We shall leave tomorrow, little warrior, to meet a bitter friend of Valerio's. For now, let us laugh, get drunk, and fall down into sleep like three dead flies."

They clashed their mugs in agreement and sat drinking in the yellow sunlight. Even serious Arruda, now slightly inebriated, joined in the laughter and silliness. All three fell into a deep, wine-sleep. They were unaware of the day's ending or the smiling passage of the midnight moon.

Morning dawned. The three companions rose and breakfasted well in each other's company.

Arruda took to finishing off some scrolls he had been occupied with. Valerio and Profeta started preparations for their journey. Valerio, full of his usual vigor, gathered their supplies and then excused himself from their company for a while.

Profeta sat and contemplated Arruda's profile as he bent over his work. Silence visited the minutes, then Profeta spoke.

"Arruda, what has sent you here? What are you always so busy writing?"

Meticulously he cleaned his brush, then lay it to dry on a flat stone.

"I, like you, came to this forest simply because I had to. I have travelled its roads for a long time just for the simple joy of it, as does Valerio. Now, I am entering a different season, and this is as it should be. After a while, one sees that the hour glass has run a little over the half way mark. One becomes more reflective of time spent adventuring and time spent with people. Everything seems to be only on loan to us; friends, life, even our own bodies. If we have been loaned so many things of miraculous value, then it seems only fitting that we somehow find a way to demonstrate a grateful heart. How we do this depends on our gifts. The times and spaces that we live in are vast. It seems I have a talent for gathering information from dimensions that, as yet, science has left untouched. Writing it all down is my own small way of contributing to times that have not yet bloomed. Imparting a little knowledge is a positive thing, but imparting wisdom is even more valuable as it may be used to make the future more profound. If I should fail, I think my time shall not be wasted, as the trying itself seems to be the thing of greater importance. Without it, there is no hope of a better tomorrow, and the trying at least makes for a better today."

"But my dear Arruda, you will grow old and dusty, looking always at your scrolls."

He smiled at her concern.

"We only grow old and dusty if we kill the child inside ourselves. How can this happen to me if I always gaze in wonder at the many things I see. I may indeed become gnarled and wrinkled, because time marches on for all of us, but never old. My eyes will always remain the eyes of a curious and amazed child."

She hugged him hard, thinking of how dear he had become to her and of how much she truly owed him.

A loud "hello" heralded Valerio's arrival. Walking and chortling to himself, he led two beautiful stallions, one ebony black the other a burnished gold. Their coats gleamed in the morning sun.

Arruda laughed out loud, while Profeta gaped in astonishment.

"Valerio, Valerio, how do you manage to procure horses at a moment's notice?"

"It is easy, Madame. One has simply to be in dire need of them, as Valerio has told you once before. The black one suits Valerio; do you not think? He shall look quite handsome upon this fine steed's back. For you, there is Duarado. Now don't look so sad, for he will give you as much pleasure as Slate. Horses come and go, you know, after their purpose has been fulfilled. As do we. Now let us be off before we become too decrepit to move."

He helped her to put the packs on the saddles. Then they mounted, ready to depart. Arruda took leave of them gently, wishing them well.

Riding and racing off, Profeta and Valerio gaily shouted back nonsense about eye strain and hen scratches. Arruda waved them off, smiling, and watched the silver streak that fluttered around Profeta's face like a banner. Soon they were out of sight. Arruda shook his head. Turning back to his scrolls and brushes, he started writing once again.

Valerio and Profeta galloped happily through the woods, laughing, singing and reveling in each other's company. By late afternoon, hunger overcame them, and they stopped at a log that lay at the side of the path.

"Where are we going, Valerio? Not that it matters much. It's such fun just travelling with you."

"Aha! Madame is trying to wheedle information from Valerio's poor, senile mind. Here, eat this bread and cheese before they mold. We, my little bird, are going to visit a friend of mine. He has had such pain in his heart, for he saw the way things were and not the way he thought things should have been for him. He grew bitter, and now he is trapped. Valerio too escaped such a trap, but long ago."

"How did you manage to escape this trap you speak of, and not he?"

"Because, Madame, Valerio knows that as lovely as he is, the world revolves quite nicely without his help. Indeed, even without his presence. The things he thinks are important often make the universe jiggle with laughter. You see the universe has a will of its own, and a sense of humor."

He paused then to wash down some cheese with a great gulp of water.

"Sometimes," he continued, "when Valerio is pompous and feels like a very clever king, the damn universe will spit in his eye. It's nothing personal, you understand, but just for the hell of it! He puffs up and roars like a lion, but then he sees the great Valerio, hopping up and down like an ineffectual child while the universe's spit dangles from his eye. Then he must burst out laughing, and the universe and Valerio become as good friends sharing a great joke together. Laughter, you see Madame, is a very simple thing. You do it like this."

He proceeded to emit great bellows, causing the woods to ring with their power. This set off Profeta, and she joined him. Their duet of mirth sounded in the dappled light, and became an elixir that sweetened their hearts, making them feel relaxed and refreshed.

"Well, eat up little piglet. There are several hours left yet to ride."

Throwing the crumbs to the birds they set off again, Profeta following Valerio. Hours passed, the trees became older and thicker. Moss and wisps of vines hung off their wooden arms. Afternoon shadows deepened. The sun hung low in the sky.

Light gave way to dusk, then darkness. They slowed their horses as the path narrowed. Eventually, they dismounted and continued their journey on foot, leading the horses single file behind them.

The low hanging branches came to a sudden stop at a small clearing, where there appeared to loom the shape of a high hedge. Valerio stopped at the obstacle.

"Madame looks tired. We will sleep here. Do not be frightened of the night. On the other side of this thicket wall dwells my friend, but on this side dwells nothing more than a colony of little brown rabbits. Valerio knows of no vicious rabbits that have ever attacked a dreaming human sort."

He chuckled as he prepared a place for them to sleep. Profeta followed his example and rolled herself up in her sleeping quilt. The day's ride had taken its toll. Soon, both were asleep.

The night breeze danced on Profeta's face. At one point, half awake, she thought she heard a thin wail carried on the wind. Valerio's light snoring floated by her fuzzy mind. Reassured, she fell back to sleep.

They woke, speckled with the morning dew. Valerio yawned and stretched. "Come laziness, let us get to the day's business."

He pulled her to her feet.

"We will leave the horses to rest, for it is but a short walk from here. We must not startle my poor friend, so we must go quietly."

They followed the border of the high hedge for about a quarter of a mile. Eventually, they came to an old, wrought iron gate. Strange symbols and rusting faces adorned it. Valerio placed a finger to his lips, stifling her questions. Wordlessly, they hurdled over the gate and jumped into a meadow beyond.

The meadow was full of cornflowers, dancing breezily on graceful stems. They pushed through the flowers slowly until they came to a small rise in the ground. They sat, not speaking, for what seemed a longish time. Valerio, all the while, watched the other side of the meadow intently.

"Ah, here he comes now," he whispered. "Do not be afraid of him, as he does harm only to himself. His soul is actually quite gentle."

She turned in the same direction and watched, fascinated, as a black form of human proportions came loping towards them from the other side of the field. As he drew closer, his features became more distinct. Profeta tried to quiet the sharp intake of her breath, for Valerio's friend was a living gargoyle.

Valerio rose slowly and walked towards him. He did not utter one word but just lay a gentle hand on the scaly back and led him back to Profeta.

The gargoyle was black as soot and, with fangs bared, snarled at her. Profeta's eyes widened in fear. She was stunned to see that he had azure blue eyes.

Seeing the silver streak in her hair, he touched it gently with his large clawed hand. Still resting his hand on her hair, he closed his eyes and let the sun lie warm on him a while. Licorice thoughts caressed his sad and savage soul. His hand moved slowly to her shoulder, then he started to guide her to the center of his meadow. He shuffled a few steps away from her, then bowed in a respectful fashion.

Profeta watched, amazed, for it seemed that he had now started to move in dance. He looked so strange and almost foolish. He was bending, spinning daintily, touching a blue petal here and there. She stood, entranced. All fear of him now dissipated. He bowed to her again as if he recognized a kindred spirit, and invited her to follow him.

Picking up the sequence of his movements, she followed his fantastic form, and the two danced together gracefully. The woman and the gargoyle. She wove and dipped with his rhythm, and her heart contracted in sympathy for this ungainly creature who now moved so beautifully.

Her eyes moved from the patterns that his feet were drawing on the ground, up to his strange and contorted face. She saw the grooves that bitterness had left behind and the untold sorrow in his eyes.

Profeta's eyes never left his face, and yet she never faltered in the gargoyle dance, not missing one beat of the silent music. She danced as if the dance was a remembered one. The world seemed to slow to their unhurried timing. The cornflowers swayed in blue parallels to the motions of their arms. When they whirled around each other slowly, it seemed to her that they melded with the axis of the spinning earth. She felt a strange unravelling in her breast, as if her heart were slowly discarding a soiled bandage, allowing the sun to dispel any sadness that had clung there. Her bitterness floated off in a grey vapor and left her to dance free.

The afternoon grew ripe and heavy. They twirled a final time, linked arms, then softly came to a halt. They bowed deeply to each other.

As if awakened from a dream, Profeta saw new cornflowers growing where their feet had woven the tapestry of their rhythm. Peaceful, her heart felt peaceful.

Valerio approached quietly. All three of them, man, woman and gargoyle stood watching the blue of the cornflowers waving under a still bluer sky.

The gargoyle lay down and fell asleep then, his mind shuttered against all thought. Valerio noticed the mauve tinge in the heavens that signaled sunset. He took Profeta's hand and pulled her to her feet, leading her without a word from the meadow and over the iron gate again.

Once out of earshot, Profeta turned to Valerio. "If your friend has bitterness from pain, then dancing in a field of cornflowers does not seem like such a horrid fate to me."

"Madame, heed Valerio's words closely. This gargoyle once was a handsome man, almost as handsome as Valerio. His cornflowers are the beauty of his pain. He guards them jealously. You danced your pain and bitterness away, clearing room for gratitude. He will not leave his pain, and so makes himself an exile in his field, where few are his visitors. He covets it. Tonight, you will see the truth of what he will not leave. We can not stay in his meadow at night, but come and Valerio will show you."

They walked a short distance until they came to a bend in the hedge. Valerio bid her hush, and formed a window where the bushes had scantier growth. They sat, watching the gargoyle as he slept a short distance away, on the other side of the bush.

Sunset came to the creature's meadow as suddenly as garnet wine spilled on white linen. Shadows of the evening, their fingers icy cold, stole into his sun-warmed heart. He became restless, then trembled, as if a film of frost had touched his soul. He felt the loneliness of dusk seep into the hollow spaces between his gargoyle bones.

Abruptly, he staggered to his feet. Violently, he shook off the remnants of his cape of sleep. He started to pace in circles, ever widening their range, as night turned the sky dark. His tortured form rose, black against the indigo sky.

Then, came the moon. Alas, he saw the Silver Queen rise on her midnight ocean. Her piercing light cast deep and forgotten memories, reflecting them in his brain. It seared with iron coldness all the peace and warmth that the sun had given him..

An exiles anguish rang out in a haunting wail across the meadow. Maddened by the visions of past remembrances, he twirled and snarled and howled at Lady Moon with tortured longing.

Profeta saw the blue of his gargoyle eyes gleam strongly. They formed chasms that travelled endlessly, to all the pain in all the world, in all of its vague disguises. The eyes started to shed tears, blue cornflower tears. The moaning night wind scattered them across the meadow, letting them fall like blue confetti to join the others growing there.

The creature's agony was terrible to see. Profeta turned her face away, wet with pity.

"Enough Valerio, I've seen enough."

He took her hand and led her back to the horses. The horror of the Gargoyle's pain came with her.

"Oh Valerio, how does he deserve this torture?"

"Think strongly Madame. He has only to leave his cornflowers to be free of it."

"Then why in heaven's name does he not leave them?"

"He clutches at his pain too strongly. He wears it like a banner across his chest. He can not hear the awful roar of the cosmos laughing. He is bitter that he feels the pain, yet can only lay blame on himself for not leaving the field."

"But Valerio, surely we can find a way to help him."

"Some have tried. Like all things, Madame, he is the only one who can hurdle the gate. Valerio feels it is too late for him. He has stayed in his field for so long that it is home to him."

"But see the night is waning. He will start to wait now, growing still. His air, his meadow, his cornflowers, all will wait now. The first thread of sunlight will soon stitch her healing pattern in to the sky. Poor friend, he did not heal properly."

They fell silent again. Each explored the private rooms inside their heads. At length, the yellow of the morning sun shook off their quietude and gave them over to happier thoughts. They sat and talked and planned into the afternoon.

Valerio had some business of his own to pursue, so Profeta decided to follow in an Easterly direction the same path that had taken them to the gargoyle's field. They packed, and then led their horses back to the main road. Valerio picked her up and set her on Durado's back. He then mounted his own black steed.

"Thank you, Valerio, for showing me your poor friend. You wise and silly man. I shall not forget all that you have taught me. If by chance you see Arruda before I do, give him my love."

Valerio looked at her long and hard.

"We shall await your return, Madame. Safe journeying. Now, don't forget to blow up Durado's nose. Don't kiss that hairy chin of his too much, though. It prickles."

He gave her horse a slap on the rump that set him to trotting. She turned back and blew her friend a kiss, then jauntily rode off. Valerio pointed his horse's nose in the opposite direction.

Silence settled in, erasing any knowledge of their visit. Profeta rode onward, more and more distance separating her and her friend.

Months passed, then years, accompanied by the sound of Durado's hoofbeats. Their travels filtered through her mind, as pictures of passing thoughts would rise to the surface to be examined. Images of past lessons glided through her, entwining with the images of the forest she was travelling through.

Introspection drifted over her like a dry leaf on an autumn wind. A feeling close to loneliness melded to her substance. She saw herself as unsettled, a nomad with no purpose. The forest's paths seemed to be passing through her life. They took her to adventures, yet gave her nothing of stability, except friendships. She rode, leaving behind both new and familiar places, and thought that it might be nice to stay in one spot. To find a purpose.

Maybe she had been wrong in saying to Arruda, so long ago, that it was enough just to travel.

A second streak of silver now adorned her hair.

Maya

One day, a subtle change in her surroundings pulled her from her reveries. The trees became sparse, and the land began to undulate. Green hills grew in height and steepness. Rectangles of green and yellow fields made an appearance. Flowering bushes with scarlet blossoms edged the road.

The road itself began to undergo a change in texture. Black cobblestones grew ever more numerous with the passing miles. The earthen quality of the path was slowly obliterated, transformed into a dark ribbon. The cobblestones made black mosaics and designs. Durado's hooves clattered on these patterns, striking a lonely sound in the late afternoon air.

Ruined houses built of rock and plaster began to dot the roadway, their lost secrets hidden by the growth of moss and grasses. Profeta wondered at their history.

She was riding up a steep grade where the road crested a hill. On reaching the top, she halted to survey the landscape and get her bearings. The road wound downwards for about two miles and ended in a settlement far below. The village lay nestled at the bottom of the hill, flanked by steep fields on three sides. The fourth side lay open to the sea. Grey and white houses followed the narrow village roadways that joined and spiraled, ending at the shoreline.

Smelling the sea air, she finished her study of the land and started a slow descent towards the village.

Reaching the outskirts, she slid off Durado's back and led him by the reigns.

The houses appeared to be silent. They had been built in long rows without flowers or grass to break the blackness of the streets, or the neutral grey and white concrete and stucco walls. At first, it seemed the place might be deserted. Then, very quietly, people in cotton robe garments started to gather. They watched silently as Profeta walked. They stared at her, then muttered amongst themselves in a strange tongue. They looked away or gave curt nods of acknowledgement when she met their open curiosity. In some of the bolder eyes, their looks seemed to hold a slight hostility, along with tinges of fear.

Feeling alien and very uncomfortable with this entourage trailing behind her, she was grateful for Durado's warm presence. She walked the long line of houses that led to the sea, feeling a great urge to run from these strange, watchful people.

The crowd stopped as she began the slow incline to the shore, still looking but no longer following her. Relieved, her feet touched the rocks, and then the warm sand. The warmth was welcome after the coolness of the cobblestones. Following the shoreline, she found a sanctuary from peering eyes behind a boulder that jutted out of a cliffside.

She sat down to collect her thoughts, and to make plans for the coming night. The sea reminded her of the place that Arruda had once taken her, but these waters were different. These had a strange, compelling pull.

The sun set royally over the horizon, and a tiny glitter marked the evening star.

"I can't stay the night here," she thought. "Maybe there is an inn somewhere in this strange village."

Turning back to face the houses, she abruptly halted. A man was picking his way towards her over the rocks. Her hand clutched Durado's mane as she waited for his approach.

He was a tall, swarthy man. He wore many years on his face with a dignified pride. Steel grey hairs and a wide moustache softened his features. He wore a robe woven of the same grey cotton as the other inhabitants, but decorated with rich purple borders.

When he drew near, he stretched out his hand in greeting. "My name is Alviro, my good woman. What brings you to the village of Maya?"

"I'm just passing through," she answered. "Would you be kind enough to direct me to some inn or shelter?"

"Maya has no inns, and the sea winds dampen the night so. Please, allow me the privilege of offering you and your horse the shelter of my humble house. I'm sure my wife will be glad of your company. It's been a long time since we had the pleasure of a visitor. May I know your name?"

"My name is Profeta. I have come from the forest. If it is small trouble, I would be grateful for the hospitality of your kind offer."

"Come then," he beckoned.

Over the rocks and sand they went and up the incline which was now deserted. They passed through the watchful streets with candlelit windows and shadowy faces. They turned up a little path away from the main street and came to a white house that overlooked the cliffside. They stabled her horse in an adjoining shed, laying out for him some sweet hay.

Alviro then opened a carved wooden door and shouted, "Natania, we have company."

A woman with posture still youthful that belied the lines on her face walked into the front room. Her expression was gentle, tempered by patience and time. Inviting Profeta to sit at a wooden table, she produced a bowl of hearty soup and warm bread.

Profeta thanked her and began to eat, while Alviro explained the circumstances of her visit to his wife.

"Well Profeta," she said. "You are welcome to stay here with us. We have a nice room with a view of the sea that you may have as your own. It is a delight to have a forest traveler with us. I suppose that the people of the village took note of your arrival?"

"They did indeed, but not knowing their language I was unable to converse with them."

"Maybe that is just as well for now," said Alviro. "Later, when things become more familiar, you will gradually learn to speak their tongue."

"But I really can't stay, save for one night. I don't see how I shall have time to learn their tongue."

Alviro and Natania exchanged a glance.

"Profeta, dear," he said, "the way out of the village is quite treacherous, unlike the way in. It may take a long time to find your way again."

"But I will simply follow the same way I came in on."

"I'm afraid dear, it's not quite that simple. First, you must understand why you came here."

"The roads out of Maya are not constant, and they are fraught with danger when they are in transition. Very few people manage to leave here, or see anything else but Maya, and a little of the surrounding countryside."

"I'm not sure that I understand all this. Is it the weather that makes the journey a danger?"

"Well dear, I could refer to it as the weather, but what I am trying to explain is this. The landscape that surrounds the village has a capacity to change; the change is not always pleasant. Being lost in the changes may well be worse than losing your life, for there is no end to the exile."

"But surely some people have made it out safely?"

"Only a very few. Explore the village life, and then decide if leaving is worth the risk."

Profeta thought in silence for a while. "I shall heed your advice," she said. "It will be a good adventure to see the village. It is fool hardy to take risks without more knowledge, and perhaps we can learn more before I set off again."

"I think you should rest now," offered his wife. "Tomorrow is time enough for worries and plans."

Profeta said goodnight to Alviro, then followed Natania down a long wooden corridor from which branched all the other rooms. Their window-eyes all peered towards the sea.

Natania ushered her into the end room. It was small but very adequate. The floor was of rough wooden planks, with white wash on all the walls. A large, latticed window opened to the sea far below. A narrow bed with wooden posts was made up with white linen and a colorful down quilt.

Natania pulled open a carved dresser drawer and handed Profeta a long, white chemise night gown. She fussed over Profeta, helping to arrange a few travel accessories on the bureau. Tucking Profeta into bed maternally, Natania blew out the candle and bid her goodnight. She then softly closed the door behind her.

Darkness fell. House noises grew silent. A lone dog barked in the village. Then nothing sounded but the constant voice of the sea, distant breakers crashing against the rocks. Profeta fell to the land of sleep.

The sound of Natania's pots broke her vessel of dreams, setting her afloat in the morning. She lay awake a while, feeling like a small girl again as she listened to the kitchen sounds. Getting up slowly, she washed in a bowl of water that was waiting for her on a chair. She then walked down the hallway to the main room and sat down at the table. She found Alviro already at breakfast.

Natania, smiling and chatting lightly, gave her a warm bowl of milk, hot honeyed bread and goat's cheese.

"Good morning Profeta." Alviro greeted her as his wife set the house to smelling of fresh coffee. "After we finish eating, we will wander down to the village and I will show you some things of interest," he said.

The three chatted throughout the meal. All the while, the older couple showed honest joy and warmth in fussing over her. Profeta, in turn, found a great affection and respect growing for them and their many kindnesses.

As promised, they set out to walk the village streets after finishing breakfast.

People in their grey robes were busy at their daily tasks. Men were carrying their implements to the near bye fields. Women dried beans in the sun, outside their houses. Children and dogs cavorted about. They all stopped to stare at Profeta, but tipped their hats cordially to Natania and Alviro, who nodded and smiled back.

Alviro paused here and there to speak with some of the people. He would introduce Profeta, and she smiled at their curious faces, studying them in turn. She noticed that in both young and old there was something of a sameness, something indescribably similar. It was as if the young were already stamped with the age to come, that this would be the same face she saw on the old. She paid heed to their obvious respect for her hosts. She also noted their great emphasis on good manners, which they used to cover their almost rude curiosity.

Alviro pointed out people and things as they walked along.

"Here is the house of the old miller. There, sitting on the step, is one of the widows. You see, she has a black border on her robe. That young girl is marrying the carpenter's son next month. The house on your right sells the finest cheese."

"Here, I must stop and speak to a man who tends gardens. You two women go ahead without me."

Alviro turned into a small house, while Natania and Profeta continued their walk. The streets held no surprises. The houses were identical, most were joined together. Only the shapes of windows and doors held any signs of individuality. The stores were in the houses, where people sold goods from front rooms.

Always, people stared at Profeta. Always, their conversations stopped as she passed by.

"Natania, why is everything so much the same here? And why do people stare at me so."

"Sameness gives these people security, which comes of no change. This is always the way that they have built their houses and worked. For them and their children, this is always the way it shall be, and it is enough for them. As for why they stare, they are intrigued and possibly a little afraid of you, because you dress and speak differently from them."

"But so do you and Alviro, yet they respect you and don't stare."

"Their respect comes from not understanding us, and perhaps from fearing us a little as well. But they are now used to our presence and have seen that we are no threat. Rather, we participate in their way of life, and so blend in to their everyday routines."

"It does seem peaceful here," conceded Profeta. "Everyone seems to have their work and their place. Do you suppose that they are happy?"

"On the whole, yes, for they have no need to question their existence. The weddings, births and deaths give them all the diversions they need. Festivals mark the repeating cycles, and unquestioned time lulls them."

"Are the festivals full of dance and music? Do they celebrate an event?"

"Most festivals are very interesting. The Black-Robed One is the master of ceremonies. In a month's time, the festival of flowers will happen. If you stay, you will see the people of Maya at one of their very important times."

"Maybe I could stay that long," said Profeta. "There may be something to learn after all." She laughed. "The fates didn't send me here for naught. After all, Maya has already given me two people that I love dearly."

She linked her arm with Natania's, and together the two slowly wound their way through the village streets, and then back to the cliffside house.

In the month that followed, Profeta continued her walks and her study of the village. A word or two of their language grew into phrases, eventually enabling her to converse with the people, on a limited basis to be sure. This sufficed nicely, for the conversations were devoid of abstract ideas, always focusing on what was at hand, revolving around the small details of everyday life.

A certain admiration filled Profeta for their ability to find peace in hard toil and small desires. She envied their contentment.

Maybe her father had been right after all. Maybe the essence of living was to be found in the things of the earth. Maybe her own joys and sorrows had been the invention of her own mind. Maybe that infernal restlessness to see more was futile.

She felt overwhelmed by a need to rest. Perhaps this Maya was a true resting place. It would be pleasant indeed to find somewhere that she could belong to so completely.

Thus were her thoughts in the indolent days that followed. Travelling was a weary way to live. How good to relax in a place where time lost its kaleidoscope of passing images, and the morning sun shone reassuringly on a little changing world.

The day of the flower festival dawned, amidst such thoughts. Scarlet blooms were picked, with great excitement, from the fields by all the villagers. They were placed in great baskets.

Later in the day, they were spread in a thick carpet, perfuming the circumference of the village.

Flags hung from the windows, ribbons and wreaths adorned the doors. An expectant air hung over the entire scene, as if awaiting the appearance of a visiting dignitary. The path of red blossoms was finally completed. The crowd, in various groups, gathered around this rosy artery of blooms.

From the center of the town was heard the rhythmic tinkling of a bell. Gathering in strength, it filled the air with tumultuous ringing, which filled and echoed in the streets.

Profeta stood in the company of Natania and Alviro. Enclosed by the crowd, they stood waiting for the better part of an hour. They waited for the festivities to begin, and the procession to advance to where they were. At mid-day, a hush suddenly fell over the crowd.

"He comes now," whispered Alviro, close in her ear.

"Who is he," she asked quietly.

Alviro answered. "The Black-Robed One. He for whom the flowers are laid."

The bells had now stopped their ringing.

He continued. "Watch carefully, but do not meet his eyes. Don't give him cause to take undo notice of you."

She was puzzled by Alviro's warning, but was unable to question him further, for their whispering was drawing attention to them.

A retinue of people approached slowly down the blossom strewn path. Four men carried a blue silk canopy over the head of the Black-Robed One. Walking with deliberate dignity, his shoes crushed the red blossoms that were under his feet. His hand held a great silver rod that glowed with a hard light as it caught the sun. The people that lined the street knelt at his passing, their faces lifted in reverie towards him. With his silver scepter, he caught the rays of the sun and reflected them into the eyes of all who gathered there. Their eyes turned milky and clouded, before they once more focused in adoration at his passing. They seemed unconscious of what had transpired. Little did they realize that he was the thief of their awareness. Little did they care, for he seemed all wise and knowing to them. .

Horrified, Profeta saw them bowing in gratitude to him. A sudden understanding of Maya and its comforting sameness crashed over her. The people stood like sheep, waiting for him to enclose their thoughts. Afraid of the responsibility that came with being individuals. Afraid of prices to be paid from being wrong, or lonely, or courageous. She saw how smug was his smile as he gazed on his population, how self righteous he looked, how self-important. He walked on the beautiful carpet, put there for him by their toil-ridden hands. It filled her with rage.

He was quite near now. As if able to sense her anger, he turned his head slowly towards her. She met his hypnotic eyes with a defiant stare. A slight twitch of annoyance played at his mouth, and his eyes slitted just for an instant. Slowly, he started to raise his scepter to reflect the sun. Before the glare could hit her retinas she raised her hands, one over the other, to shield her sight from his power. The ray struck her flesh, scorching both hands.

The Black-Robed One had not missed a step. He continued past her. He did not glance at Alviro or Natania, who were standing close beside her. The devotees were oblivious to what had transpired, and looked respectfully at his receding back.

Following a curve in the row of buildings, he disappeared from view. The flowers he had trodden on had already lost their color. Only a hint of crimson could be seen amongst the wilted brown. His passing had brought death to their natural splendor. Gently, the sea wind started to scatter them over the cobblestones and bared once more the dark designs of the patterned streets beneath.

Profeta trembled. Chilled, her hands felt heavy and swollen. She sensed Natania's arm around her, steering her gently towards the house.

A bitter anger at both the Magician and the people made her unable to speak. Alviro ushered her into the house. Tenderly, he looked at her charred hands. He then rose to retrieve a jar from one of the cupboards. Taking out some red kelp, he layered it over the burns and blisters. The plants soothed the pain almost immediately. When the look of suffering left her face, he spoke.

"Ah Profeta, you should have heeded my advice. Now that he is angered, you will have to leave Maya quickly, and too soon. There is no time to adequately prepare for such a perilous journey. You have offended his pride, and now he will set the villagers against you. They will be incited by anger and fear. At first, they will return to ignoring you, but slowly they will begin hunting you like a pack of jackals. You will become the personification of all the evil that he warns them about. Because they are not strong, they will hate you for your show of strength. The weak can become very cruel when secure in numbers. Your hands will heal with this sea plant, but then you must leave. Very soon they will gather in a mob, inciting each other into hatred."

Profeta looked earnestly at Alviro.

"Everything is happening so quickly. I barely understand the events. Tell me, what makes you so different from the rest? Why did he not force his ritual on you and Natania? Why do you not leave? You are not a part of these mindless people."

He looked at his wife who nodded in assent. "Natania and I were also forest dwellers, not so long ago," he admitted. "In our travels, we came across a scroll, written by the scholar Arruda. It told of this place."

Profeta started at the familiar name, but kept silent and listened.

"The scroll had in it wisdom, and incantations that work against the Black-Robed One. He, in turn, knows that we possess it. Therefor he does not bother us. If he does, in the ensuing battle he would run the risk that one of the people born of the village might come into possession of the scroll. That, dear one, would be the end of his power. He will be glad when we are gone."

Alviro chuckled.

Now Natania continued. "You see, young friend, though we were not born of these people, we chose to come. In our travels, we have seen many places. Here, the incline to the sea pleases us. We have come for a little peace in our lives before our final journey."

Profeta looked at the acceptance in their faces. "Surely there is a better place to melt into the sea's infinite dimensions than this?"

"But it is as good a place as any. In all places, there are magicians who wish to steal your will. It is not always possible to study every way to keep oneself safe from a myriad of creatures such as he. Another magician could just be too strong for us. We are, after all, just a little dust on this planet. This one, at least, is in no position to torment our last days.

Profeta spoke up. "Shouldn't you free the others? What of their freedom? Is it not unjust to keep the secrets of the scroll solely for yourselves?"

"Unjust, you say? What a nebulous word is justice. How it can change from whatever position one takes. Think of the grave responsibility. What favor would we do them if they were forced to start journeying? They are not yet strong enough to fight the changing landscapes that surround this place. If they were strong enough, it would have happened already, naturally. By forcing them to see another way, would it truly be a kindness? Or would it just be a stand taken to show that we are right, and they are wrong."

"They are at heart good people, but nearly all of them would go mad, seeking their peace on some misty ground they have not experienced. Bereft of stability, they would only drown in other illusions, dangerous as quicksand. Those who could make it will go anyway. The rest are content now."

"Before they find their rest in the sea, their eyelids may be torn open, revealing his magic and bringing just a momentary flash of pain that will pass quickly."

"If their eyes were to open to freedom now, before they have ripened in reality, then their pain could well last all of their lifetimes. And even then, truth might still not be within their reach. They may go totally blind, groping through life until the sea could give them peace."

"It is different for us. We consciously chose to travel, and then to come here. Would we not just be another black magician to them, forcing them into something they are not prepared for?"

"Don't be saddened child," added Natania. "It will all change when the time deems fit. From inside will come the change, as all changes to growth do. But enough talking now. Alviro, we must heal her hands and plan her departure out of Maya."

Profeta had no need of further encouragement, for a great fatigue overcame her. Gratefully she went to her bed, a dull throb in her hands and a great need to rest her mind. Gladly, she left the details of her escape to her wiser companions.

Natania and Alviro left her to sleep throughout the night and into the next day, while they prepared her provisions and her horse for the journey. They looked in on her now and again. Natania stroked the two streaks of silver in Profeta's hair as it lay tousled on the pillow.

They woke Profeta in the late afternoon, Alviro removed the red kelp from her hands and was satisfied with its work. The hands were healed, with no scars to mar their life lines. Natania had Profeta's garments packed, her travelling cape and quilt mended. There was nothing left to do save to enjoy one last meal in each other's company. Their talk was subdued and solemn, as befitted Profeta's danger and the farewell to come.

When Alviro had finished eating, he went to the window to get a good view of the village below. His face was grave as he turned back to the women.

"Profeta, you must leave before sunset. I see the villagers gathering with torches at the courtyard of his mansion. They will surely come at the beginning of nightfall, before the moonrise. You must be out on the changing road by then."

"I will go as you advise, Alviro. Will the same road I took into the village take me back to the forest?"

"You can not use that road, for they will seek you out on it until you are out beyond the outlying fields. It will be too risky, for they know all the shortcuts and may try to waylay you before the land goes into transition. No, you must leave by another path. I will show you one. It follows an Eastern trajectory. The changes come sooner, but it is the only way to ensure your physical safety. Whichever way you go, you must still pass through those landscapes."

"You keep speaking of these changes. How does the land change? What course must I follow?"

"How it will change for you I can not tell, for that always depends on the individual. The only course one can take is to not trust anything. Until you can hear the sea, keep on in the direction you are heading. Never wander off the road or change course. No matter what happens, Profeta, do not step one foot off the path. It is the only way to keep your balance, and not be forever lost. Remember this, for the way is treacherous. Do not be fooled by images or terrors, as these dwell in your mind only. Think of where you are going; you have to go alone. Staying the course will take you to the sea, and on to your forest. I will show it to you now, for soon the sun will set."

"I will stay here," said Natania. "If the villagers come, as they surely will, I shall tell them that you left by the main road, and that Alviro is tending his fields. They do not have the power within them to question deeply, and the Black-Robed One will not come with them for the hunt."

Profeta rose and exchanged an embrace with the older woman. After a moment, they held each other at arm's length, their eyes moist. Natania broke away and turned to a closet in the kitchen. She took from it a beautiful oaken staff and presented it to Profeta.

"Take this as your own. Alviro carved it for me from a felled oak tree, many years ago. Alas, I have no further use for it, but it has been a good companion to me. It has kept me safe at times, and I have leaned on it when I became weary. Hush now, and don't interrupt an old woman. Take it as your own, I say"

Profeta felt the smooth wood in her hands, the weight and balance of it, its warm heaviness. Her eyes filled with gratitude. She clasped the woman's hands to her bosom and kissed them. Then, she watched silently as Natania took her leave and went back into her kitchen.

Profeta did not trust herself to speak. She turned to follow Alviro to where Durado stood. Leading the horse, the two of them walked around the little house to the small garden, then through a quiet orchard and onto the adjoining hillside. They were soon hidden from view by the scarlet shrubs that bordered the fields. Steadily climbing, they finally crested the swell. Alviro led her a short distance further, through an empty meadow.

The village was now hidden behind the hill. Presently, their feet found an overgrown path that wound its way further downhill in an Easterly direction. It was paved with the familiar black cobblestones.

"It is here that we must part company. Remember, do not leave the road Profeta!" Alviro's voice was stern as he warned her once more.

"I won't, Alviro," she answered. "Will I ever see you and Natania again?"

"Who knows. Perhaps in the sea's foam," he said wistfully. Don't let this trouble you now. Friends stay forever with us, even if the meeting is brief. After all, life's gifts are only on loan, as is life itself. Go now, with firm resolve. Natania's staff and your horse will be your trusted companions, and will guide you well."

He kissed her forehead. She hugged him tightly, then mounted Durado. Their eyes met and held for a moment. All was silent, but for their smiling sadness at leave-taking. He slapped Durado on the rump to startle him into a canter.

She turned back to wave at Alviro before the shrubbery hid him from sight. Then, brushing the hair from her eyes, she nudged Durado into a brisk trot down the roadway.

After a few miles of riding, the urgency of putting distance herself and her pursuers lessened as no one seemed to be following her. Her senses observed everything with sharp acuity, as she did not know what to expect on this road after all of Alviro's warnings. The rose tint that remained in the sky appeared quite normal as it reflected over the hills. Thinking that Alviro might have been mistaken as to the danger of the path, she slowed to a walk.

"Perhaps he fell prey to superstitions," she thought.

Birds were chattering, preparing for nightfall. The sound mixed pleasantly with the rustling of the breeze through the foliage.

The pink light in the sky was eventually extinguished, and evening fell like a dark satin cloak, with the wind sighing in its slippery folds.

Horse and rider were approaching a long stretch of open grasses, and no hedges or trees outlined the dark horizon. There was just the open field, levelling into the night sky.

The sound of a cricket chirping floated through the air, followed by another. Soon, the field came alive, growing louder as she rode closer. As she came abreast of their orchestra, the cacophony grew even stronger until it obliterated any other sounds. It started to beat on her ear drums with an uncanny, high vibration.

She grew uneasy. Glancing down at Durado, she saw only the usual twitching of his ears. She thought herself foolish for becoming agitated by the sound of insects.

She finished her passage through the open country, feeling relieved when the sounds began to fade.

Suddenly, they stopped altogether. She became unnerved at the abruptness of their silence. A chill fell on the air and she drew her cloak more tightly around her. She felt small and vulnerable in the darkness yet did not dare to leave the road for a hiding place.

No stars twinkled in the night sky, and the time had not yet come for the moon to rise.

Profeta nervously scanned the landscape. Her darting eyes saw only outlines of inanimate rocks and quietly rustling vegetation. Stopping Durado, she listened to the night. Blood rushed in her ears with every beat of her heart. The quiet wind reached her as if from far away.

"It is the silence that brings with it this strange foreboding," she thought.

The creeping silence was becoming a cold and tangible thing. Its negative space started to swell and bloom around her like a black rose. She stood transfixed as the dark petals caressed, then enveloped her senses. The world shrank, and her eyes dilated to better search the darkness.

She knew no one but she alone was there. That "aloneness" snaked a curling, cold tendril around her heart. This left her gasping, impaled on thorns of loneliness.

A pain in her diaphragm gave birth to a dark universe. It seeded there, and sucked like a leech at any love of life it found. Melancholy bubbled in. It rose into her being and filled her with panic, fragmenting her logic until naught remained but the cold empty spaces found between stars and uninhabited black holes.

There she stayed, trapped. No warmth, no light. Alone.

"Fada." Her mouth opened in a silent scream. It broke and floated like a bubble of black molasses towards the empty sky.

The darkness nudged a thin, hesitant moon into giving off a watery light. A faltering blessing to stricken eyes, unseeing, blind to joy. Reflected in her stony tears, a prism where strangled sounds ushered up a thousand images of the self-exiled Gargoyle screaming in his field. A thin wail came, like a needle, from her throat.

"Madness," she panted. "Lonely madness."

She jumped from her horse and gazed in desperation at the welcoming darkness that lay like a sleeping reptile at the edge of the road. It goaded her to run into its ink, looking for surcease from her sorrow.

Finding her voice, she screamed at the night. Clutching her staff with white knuckles, she sought to overcome the compulsion to run off the road.

Gathering her trembling limbs, she tore at her memory to find there buried the intricate steps of the Gargoyle's dance. With unsteady feet and madly gesturing arms, she dipped, turned jerkily and twisted into the forms that the Gargoyle had taught her. Ungainly and jerking were her movements at first, as if a broken puppet dangled from its strings. Then, oh so very gradually, she slowly found the rhythm of her wild and irregular pulse.

After an infinite amount of time, the wildness of her frenzy started to ebb, leaving her movements to once again find their natural grace. The marble whiteness in her cheeks gave up their pallor, turning pink from her exertions. Breath slowly normalized.

She became aware of her garments, which stuck damply to her moving limbs. Slowly, the precipice she had started her dance on receded. Her feet, now firm, patterned the dance into the strange designs of the cobblestones.

The burden of loneliness began to transform as she became more aware of her own moving being. A calm stillness began to spread from the center of her body to her limbs and mind. She knew then that this quiet within was always there, right beside the friend of self. The night had disguised it as the terror that had attacked her so horribly, but in a flash of understanding she knew that the terror was within her own being also. The urge to run from the road and hide in the fields was gone.

Her motion was slowing, unwinding. Graceful as a cornflower she swayed to a stop, her face upturned to the early dawn sky.

Profeta stood, quiet and exhausted. The image of the rising sun played over her features, as the ruddy stain of its rebirth gave way to a golden, living light. She put her face near Durado's warm nose and inhaled his breath.

Her heart was still. Once more it beat peacefully.

Feeling very tired, Profeta heaved herself back into the saddle, pulling strands of damp locks from her cheeks. Bemused, her fingers tangled in the two silver streaks of hair that lay on her shoulders.

Thus, her first night on the road out of Maya came to an end.

Her slow ride began again. Profeta now appreciated how essential it was to keep her balance on this fantastic travel to the sea. Riding, always keeping to the road, she longed for it to end, longed for the song of the sea and the familiarity of her forest.

Tiredness claimed her. Tiredness from this journeying, tiredness from always having to be wary, tiredness from not being able to guess what perils the road held. A great need for sleep overcame her. The sun was scribing a slow arc in the sky, and its warmth filled her with lassitude. Eyelids became droopy, full of thick, warm, honey sunshine. The steady, monotonous sound of Durado's clopping hooves beat a staccato rhythmically on her tired brain.

On she rode, feeling more and more disembodied as the hours stretched into mid-day. The sun's rays melded from soft gold into a harsh, white light, bleaching the land and pouring a black, tarry sheen on the road. Mirages danced in waves across her squinting, weary eyes. Listless and dozy, she watched the glare on the road, unblinking. The torpor and empty stare of a lotus eater fell on her consciousness like a veil. All became stagnant and sluggish.

Somnambulant she rode, letting the reigns fall slack, unheeding, giving Durado a free head. Sun glare had hypnotized her, fatigue the only thing left within, her body now a burden to her breathing. Too tired she was to turn her head, too tired to think. Only energy enough to stare at the hypnotic globe of light ahead, torching the road with its burning.

Profeta plodded relentlessly towards it. Her eyes past caring, unblinking. She felt her sight being pulled to the center of the light, obeying its gravity. The road curved sharply, but the blazing sphere shone straight ahead, off the road and into the barren fields.

A small, red bird zig-zagged across her line of vision. Her nearly dormant brain recalled the Black-Robed One's scepter, and a warning buzzed as if in a dream. She knew that she must close her eyes to block out the glare, but all control over her lids was gone. They seemed to be stuck open.

Only three feet were left before the edge of the road. Her staff fell, clattering on the stones, awakening self-preservation. Her weighted, leaden arms started to lift. Her body, fighting an ocean of exhaustion, tried to raise them higher. Muscles knotted and cramped. Sweat beaded her brow and upper lip. Fighting the ache with all of her might, she managed to palm her eyes just as Durado's next step would have taken them off the road.

Turning her head, she looked at her staff, lying on the cobblestones below her horse. Her mind, like an arrow, found its way back to her command. With a sharp pull to the right, she reigned Durado's head back to the center of the road.

Shaken by the closeness of their danger, she realized that fatigue was a luxury she could ill afford.

As Profeta dismounted and retrieved her staff, she noted that the sphere of light was no longer there. The sun was getting lower in the sky, losing its intensity.

She unpacked her quilt, then tied Durado's reigns to her wrist. Then she slept on the hard cobblestones until the second night turned its pages into the second dawn.

Feeling stronger in the morning, she decided that it would be best to walk, and lead Durado by the reins, thus keeping herself awake. After a mile or so, her aches were disappearing, and her fatigue had dissolved.

She took new interest in her surroundings. Hillsides were rising higher now, forming sharper angles. Black boulders, the same shade as the cobblestones, jutted abruptly into the windings of the road.

Off the path a way, a large, blue lizard lay sunning itself on one of the rocks, its yellow pupils watching the passing of Profeta and her horse. This small sign of life reassured Profeta and returned a sense of optimism.

A jagged, black crag thrust its way onto the path. While skirting it, she heard a thin wail rising high in the air. It came from some unknown source. She halted her steps to investigate. There, huddled against a rock just at the edge of the road, was a small, very thin, naked girl. Strangled, bubbling sobs came from deep within her little chest.

"How horrible to be lost in this desolate and dangerous country," Profeta thought.

Her heart immediately reached out to the little one's plight, ignoring the detail that the child was huddled off the roadway, and alone. Profeta knelt and opened her arms in a universal gesture to the small infant. Like a little rocket, the girl hurtled herself into the welcoming arms, and was gathered up in one easy motion.

Trembling and cold, she pressed herself hard against Profeta's warmth.

Attempts made to elicit a verbal response from the child brought nothing but mewling, guttural sounds.

"Poor tiny thing," soothed Profeta. "What ill fortune you must have suffered, wandering alone and unprotected in a place like this. Do not fear, little one. I'll take you with me from this cursed land. You are safe now. Durado is strong enough to carry the both of us." She mounted her horse, cooing to the child in a quiet voice.

The girl lay in Profeta's arms, gazing up at her with pale, golden eyes, victimizing her heart. Hugging her a little closer, Profeta formed protective wings with her cape around the small burden.

It was good to feel the warmth against her breast. The child seemed content, gently touching Profeta's face and playing with the silver in her hair, until sleep overcame her. The tiny being was a comfort to Profeta, adding strength to her resolve to get to the sea and bringing a protective instinct to her heart.

Night came upon them. Profeta stroked the curve of the child's cheek as she lay sleeping. Breathing evenly, she let fall a relaxed arm around Profeta's waist.

"Sleep well, little one," she thought. She covered the child completely with her cape so the night air would not make her cold.

Profeta continued for several hours into the night. A curtain of clouds had hidden the moon and stars in the soft drape of the heavens.

The eternal black rocks hemmed the two of them in uneven shadows. They rode on for several more hours, in this passage of hard darkness.

Profeta's thoughts were interrupted by a small itch at her waist. She shifted in the saddle, seeking relief, but the bothersome, prickly feeling persisted. Holding the girl in one arm, she sought to touch the spot and alleviate her discomfort.

Thinking some small insect was trapped within her clothing, she gently edged her fingers under the child's hand to still this minor irritation. Her hand touched across a tiny, sharp object at the end of the small, curled fingers. Still wishing to protect the girl from the night chill, she turned up the hem of her cloak that covered the little hand.

Horror and disbelief! Transfixed, Profeta saw blue, scaly skin that erupted into sharp claws. Tearing her cape from the form lying in her lap, her eyes met those of a Lilith glaring at her in hatred. It began to laugh at her, the shrill laugh of one half mad.

In the split second of time that Profeta sat, unnerved, the creature hurtled itself at her neck. It razed the skin with its talons. Survival came to the forefront, as Profeta felt beads of blood tickling her neck and felt the pain of thorns in her flesh. Instinctively, she grabbed at its scrawny, pathetic throat. Her terror powered a relentless squeeze on the wheezing windpipe. Its arms flailed wildly, trying to rip at Profeta's face. Such was the wild creatures hate that even as it struggled for life, it could not give up the drive to cause her harm.

She squeezed harder until the Lilith's eyes began to bulge and a gurgling, choking sound emanated from its throat. The face and body transformed under her hands into the little girl-child, hissing piteously for air. Her eyes pleaded for release from the painful pressure. Caught in the fabulous, non-substantive net of these changing realities, Profeta's body did not respond to her mind any longer. Her action, born of fright and revulsion, sought out its own completion.

She felt the creature's windpipe shatter, but still could not command her hands to stop until the small body lay limp and lifeless.

Nausea rose up in her throat at her own capacity for violence. Her mouth filled with bile. She focused her eyes on the child that she had just murdered. Instead, a lizard lay limply in her hands, its scaly flesh soft and bulky in her hands. She threw it from her, and it hit a rock with a small thud.

Profeta vomited then, retching violently on the roadway.

As the sun rose on the third day of her journey out of Maya, she understood that compassion without wisdom was indeed an ever-present danger.

Day broke the nightmare. Jig-saw puzzle thoughts fled like ravens, stilling and quieting her mind. Questioning events in this place was futility itself. Logic fast became the way to madness here, a useless tool on these cobblestones. Intellect was the queen dethroned, for balance came from another realm. For this moment, now, Durado and the road were the only reality.

The earth now became nothing but black lava stones. The never-ending road led still deeper into the labyrinth. The shadows of the eerie rock cast a great oppression over Profeta and would not leave her for miles and miles. An ethereal burden slouched on her shoulders, a burden without name that seeped from the stone landscape. Thus, she rode on.

When next she fixed her eyes to scan the horizon, a huge shape floated into her vision. A high, black mountain loomed ahead. The road wound relentlessly towards it; past archways hollowed by the fluttering wind, through crevices that time had slashed into the land, around the shiny boulders that jutted in the way. Profeta looked with grave trepidation at the direction that the road was leading.

Upon reaching the base of the mountain, the road climbed steeply by very narrow switchbacks, all the way to the summit. On one side, a sheer, smooth drop to rocks below. On the other, a glistening, smooth wall that reached to the very heavens.

By skirting around this mountain, she could reach the same point in the road, without the risk of falling to her doom. She weighed the possibilities.

If Durado lost his footing, or if she panicked, they could fall. There would be a terror filled eternal second before death could take her on its crashing wing.

Leaving the road, however, might bring eternal terrors. Far worse than the fear of death, they would trap her for untold ages in madness.

Agonizing over the decision did no good, for the answer was not found in logic. In the end, the matter was quite simple.

"There is no choice, Profeta," she whispered softly to herself. "Fate has decided the path you must follow. Don't let the mistake of doubt creep into your soul. Use faith to journey over the mountain. Faith in yourself, in Durado, in Fada. 'Faith is a very tangible force, that stills the baying of the watch dogs of the intellect.'" Arruda had described faith in this way, once, in conversation.

Letting out a deep breath, she started up the treacherous climb. She stilled her own fears by murmuring encouragement in Durado's ears, straining not to look down as the security of that which was earth steadily receded away.

Nor could she look up at where they were going, as the dizzying heights brought no comfort. The solid wall of rock, looming oppressively on her right, gave the impression that it was trying to push her off her mount.

She forced her shoulders down, and concentrated on breathing in her belly.

Gradually, her ears began to pop as she gained altitude. Stiffening with the fear of falling, she again felt her heart contract. She knew that one thin thread of fate pulled at the string of her heart's final beat.

"The sky," she thought. "I'll focus on the sky for a while."

But peace did not come, for the rising height made the clouds loom closer. Durado's back hoof loosened a stone, which clattered down the mountainside so far that it passed into soundlessness. Knowing that her tension would translate to Durado, and ultimately could cause an error in his footing, she once again forced her shoulders down and concentrated on her breathing. Her eyes she rested solely on her horse's mane.

Hours seemed to pass, marked by the slow and steady sound of her stalwart horse's hooves.

A fine cold mist teased at her face, then got increasingly thicker. She was now at the level of the gossamer clouds. Sightless she was for a while, as the whiteness of the mist grew thicker, leaving her with no trace of her surroundings.

Profeta's breath began to quicken as the atmosphere thinned.

She voyaged on through the nebulous, cold haze until she finally broke through the clouds. Now, her eyes could see only sky with its penetrating blue sharpness. A sky so blue, it was a forever sky. That thin line at the edge of space. The clouds were now rolling white hills lying beneath her.

They had reached the summit; Her breathing had become more difficult. She paused now to look around. Cupped in the summit, just ahead and to the side, was a cavern. It seemed a kind of shelter, made for a wayfarer such as she. The road widened to become the floor of the cavern, flat and glistening like a polished jet.

Deciding to rest a while, she slid off Durado's back. She stepped along the smooth, glass-like rock and into the shallow cave. Inside, she sat with her staff beside her. She tried not to think of where her journey might end, or surmise when the blessed time would come when she would once more be in the green forest. The outline of

Durado, silhouetted against the cavern's opening, gave comfort to her tired eyes. To shut them was a small gift.

She felt the rock against her back, its strength felt smooth and cool. The fisherman of slumber cast his net deep into her mind and caught the images dancing there. Tightening the net, he drew her into sleep.

Profeta's slumber was short lived. A knife, sharp as a surgeon's steel, cut through the nets of sleep that lay upon her. The blade, a silken whisper in her ear. None other had that sound but Silvamalo's tongue. Grabbing her staff, she jumped to her feet in terror, shrinking back against the wall.

This was no dream. Silvamalo stood there facing her, his handsome face full of concern and a longing in his eyes.

"I have such pain," he whispered. "I've had no rest since losing you."

His features were contorted, reminiscent of the pain that the Gargoyle's eyes had held. A pain that had filled her with pity, in that meadow so long ago.

She wanted to protect Silvamalo from that grieving. Guilt snaked slowly into her heart, for she felt that it was she who had caused his anguish.

"I followed you my love, all of this dangerous way. I beg you to bring salve to my heart, and to end my misery with just a few kind words from you."

An overwhelming urge to comfort him filled her. She was about to throw down her staff and embrace him, when a scuttling came from within the shadowed rocks. A Lilith's face peered out at them from the gloom. Silvamalo's eyes fluttered for one instant from Profeta's to the jealous Lilith and the spell was broken. She saw his true face, stripped of loving words. Hard and insincere, his lines were cruel. He was the keeper of lies.

Valerio's lesson now came back to her; the strongest opponent is ourselves. She saw once more how silken words lay traps for pitying hearts.

"You are a liar, Silvamalo! The agony within your eyes was only pain that I would feel. You are a liar, and liars rob the light from those who would listen. You are a darkness."

"Have pity on me, Profeta. Have pity on my soul, if not my heart. Help me find my way to light again. You could show me how to change."

"I have no strength to loan you, Silvamalo. If change is what you truly wish, then find your way to it. Is truth so very hard to speak?"

Silvamalo's face betrayed impatience at this turn in the conversation. An impotent rage started to brew inside of him. He could not believe that a puny woman-creature would not succumb to his pity or his charm.

"Come, take my hand, Profeta," he said, stepping towards her.

She took two running steps out of the cave to escape his outstretched hand. Her back was to the mountain's edge. She stood facing him, silently now. Her staff was relaxed and ready in her hands, the point following his movements.

The wind outside the cave began to blow hot and dry. Silvamalo edged towards her with his hand still outstretched, pleading in his voice. The wind picked up in force and whirled around her, blowing his words like so much scattered paper on the air.

Calm and cold, she focused on his face, the words no longer holding any power. The wind continued to rip the words from Silvamalo's mouth, leaving nothing but a face unmasked and full of stalking cunning.

Now, he mouthed obscenities at the wind. His eyes became slits full of hatred. Profeta remained relaxed, still focused on his face, no flicker of emotion interrupted her guard.

She could now intuit his intentions as they started to form, for her own mind was very still. As if in slow motion he made a lunge for her, hoping to thrust her over the mountain's edge. She easily sidestepped his onslaught, holding him at bay with her staff.

Blind now with rage, he rushed at her once more. Her back was now to the cave, as she sidestepped once again. This time, she brought her staff around her head in a great arc, cracking him in the open ribs.

His face contorted with pain and anger. With all his strength he made a run towards her, hands held like claws before him, itching to bring about her demise.

She waited with a calmness that belied the graveness of her position.

The second that he was within range, she thrust the point of her staff directly at his neck with all her might. Her weapon met its mark.

His hands grabbed for his neck and he stumbled. The wind whipped his cloak over his face, and with its invisible force tipped the scale of Silvamalo's precarious balance. With one final look of sheer horror, it seemed like he flew over the edge, careening into space. His claws, that had seemed so threatening only moments before, now seemed so feeble as they thrashed at the empty air.

He screamed out her name in terror. "Profeta!" echoed off the cave walls, then fell into silence as if the sound were a fly hitting the glass walls of a jar. Then nothing but the howling of the wind.

She stood there pale and shaken, but resolute. Wind flapped at her robes, grabbed at her hair and impeded her steps towards her waiting, restless horse. With difficulty, she flung herself into the saddle and began her descent against the constant raging of the wind.

Clouds now hid the small time of light between day and nightfall. Black ribbons of darkness were tossed in the strange tides of the heaving air. The wind's voice grew ever stronger, drumming in Profeta's ears. She tried yelling over the din, but it ripped her voice from her mouth and flung all but its own sound into soundlessness.

She desperately urged Durado onward. The roaring began to splinter off in a great cacophony of onrushing tones, screaming at the descending horse and rider. Strong vibrations filled her skull, tearing away all thought, rattling every bone, bursting like a shattered mirror into a myriad of sounds.

She rode still faster down the dangerous path, followed by all the sounds that the earth's dimensions could emit: thin wailing, elusive music, sighs of passion, laughter, roaring cannons, tortured screams, cooed comfort, feet thumping on stone floors, the ramblings of the insane, pleas for mercy, angry shouts, words of defiance. All the sounds of the universe caught in the whirlwind. It was a vortex of pain and awe full beauty, all the opposites dancing in the wild cosmic winds of life's dichotomy. The four directions of all human hearts, and their raucous music flung on all four winds, blowing against the woman and her horse. She was forced to listen to all its joy and sorrow, all the awesome splendor of the great symphony of being.

And thus, the last night out of Maya was spent.

As the forth day dawned, the sounds began to unite once more, becoming less discordant. The wind began to calm itself again into a benevolent breeze. She was almost at the bottom of the mountain, her face turned to the East.

Subtly, so subtly that not one note gave away the flow, of one sound mingling with another. The wind shifted and almost imperceptibly changed into the rhythmic sound of the sea. So natural was the change that it was beyond the realm of the ear. It was now definitely the sea calling to her, calling from the boundaries of her beloved forest.

She spurred Durado into a full gallop down the road, gliding smoothly over its patterns and symbols. She felt a great rush of joy at the site of warm, black sand along the edge of the sea. Here, abruptly ended the road out of Maya.

The morning sun caught the three silver strands that now decorated her hair. She slipped of Durado and began walking the thin, hard line of sand, feeling the ocean's froth tickling her feet. Walking set her mind turning slowly, grinding out past events on the heavy millstones of memory. She walked back over the tapestry of her life's pattern, all the way back to the lilac dell.

Arruda's wisdom came to her, as well as the joyous and courageous spirit of her friend Valerio. How much older she seemed to herself now. The road out of Maya had indeed changed her. Her innocence was gone.

A sadness overtook her then. She slowed her steps and sat down in the sun. The sea washed the shore, washed her mind, and made her sleep.

She slept, a dreamless time until the day lost its warmth. Awakening, she sat motionless and watched the setting of the sun. Twilight descended, and the tide ebbed.

The evening star hung in a chiffon sky. Profeta unfolded herself, walking to a small pool left behind by the retreating tide and washed her face. The sweet smell of cedar and spruce mingled with the salt air, coming in gusts. The scent of nostalgia.

A silver glint reflected on the water, revealing the moon's face as it rose shining over her right shoulder. She caught her own reflection in the little pool. Small lines were etched around her eyes, where none had been before. Three silver streaks decorated her hair. There was also a strength in the line of her jaw, a straight and unfaltering gaze in her eyes. Studying this new face, she sat still and calm.

A drop of spray fell into the little mirror-pond, breaking the surface into small concentric circles. Countless images of herself floated uneasily across the pool.

There, superimposed, was her beloved green lady smiling up at her. Only for an instant did the image stay, leaving Profeta's face once again reflected on the now still water.

She put her hand thoughtfully into the pool and pulled out a green strand of seaweed. It had the salty smell of the sea and the texture of long, fine hair.

Smiling softly to herself, Profeta sat bemused. She held the strand of seaweed in her hand until the light of the morning crept over the sand, followed by the oncoming tide.

Profeta stood up, a lightness in her motion and a feeling of spaciousness in her heart. She led Durado to the outskirts of the forest.

As she set foot through the first line of trees, a voice loud and clear startled her.

"Well, Madame has finally decided to return to her long-suffering friends after so many years of gross neglect. We have been pining, and shriveling like weeds without water for lack of your presence."

Profeta burst out laughing in joyous delight. "Valerio, Valerio, you crazy man. I see your girth has grown, for all your talk of shriveling. Have I been gone for long? It seems like only a passage of days."

"The sands of time fall in relative patterns. How can you say that my girth has grown? It is merely maturity that I wear on my belt, and it makes the women go mad with longing."

Profeta laughed again.

"Valerio, you and your tales of women never change. Listen, my friend, do you think that Arruda would teach me how to use the scrolls and brushes?"

"We shall seek out the old hermit professor and see if he will divulge to you his little secrets. He is but a half day's ride away. It was he who sent Valerio to meet you."

"Who told him of my arrival?"

"Madame, I see that you still question what just is."

"You are right, Valerio. There is such sacred magic in the everyday that it should no longer surprise me. It is just the way of things."

They rode off into the green forest to find their friend, chatting as if no time had passed between the then and now of their last farewell.

Unseen, in the pale blue spaces beyond the earthly image of the sky, the planets and stars moved and rotated in their silent sailings. The pull of their gravities went unfelt by Profeta, her friends, or the other journeying men and women who wandered in the green of that living wood.

Special thanks to Nancy Boyes and Chris Parry,
you know what you did,
also Judith Mackey Stirt
for her artistry and encouragement.

Printed in Canada